sammy keyes

AND THE sisters of mercy

Also by Wendelin Van Draanen

How I Survived Being a Girl
Sammy Keyes and the Hotel Thief
Sammy Keyes and the Skeleton Man

sammy keyes

AND THE sisters of mercy

by WENDELIN VAN DRAANEN

SCHOLASTIC INC.

New York Toronto London Auckland Sydney
Mexico City New Delhi Hong Kong

ISBN 0-439-06507-0

12 11 10 9 8 7 6 5   2 3 4/0

Printed in the U.S.A.   40

First Scholastic printing, November 1999

To the woman who knocked on my door looking for a jacket, and walked away with one...and a piece of my heart.

Special thanks to those colleagues at St. Joseph High School
who have given me encouragement and support, especially
Dave Siminski, Greg Sarkisian, Toni Jetter, Brenda Curlee,
Phyllis Sabo, Sheila Zierman, Lanny Ahler, Susan Schmitt,
Sharon Domingues, Ann Morris, Elizabeth Gregory,
and Barbara Rieger. Thanks, too, to Greg, Dave, Sheila,
Staci Cochiolo, and Jim Armstrong for their technical
advice and help with research.

Also, thanks, as always, to Mark and Nancy.
Where would I be without you?

sammy keyes

AND THE sisters of mercy

PROLOGUE

**I was supposed
   to be in church
   to get myself
      out of trouble.**

Not to pray my way out, like most people. No, to *work* my
way out. It's a long story, but I was doing time at St.
Mary's because Vice Principal Caan thought twenty hours
of community service was a good way to make up for the
way I'd used and abused the school's PA system.

And really, I didn't mind. Helping Father Mayhew in
the church after school was a whole lot better than detention. Trouble is, while I'm in the middle of scrubbing dirt
off Baby Jesus' stained-glass face, Father Mayhew discov-
ers that something's just been stolen.

And the only people in the church are him—and me.

1

ONE

Father Mayhew isn't the kind of man you'd ever steal from. And it's not because he's big and blustery or mean, because he's not. It's because he's priestly. Now, lots of priests walk around during the day *acting* holy, but when they're all alone, there's no doubt about it—they pick their noses and burp and pass gas just like you and me.

Not Father Mayhew. Well, okay, maybe he burps now and then, but you can bet he says, "Excuse me!" to God when he does it. The point is, Father Mayhew is holy. Very holy. He walks with a glow, if that makes any sense, and he never raises his voice. Ever.

I think part of the reason he never raises his voice is because of his accent. He's Irish and his A's and R's kind of roll around in his mouth a bit before they come out. That, and he says lad and lass a lot, so he always *sounds* friendly, even when he's talking about burning in Hell.

Father Mayhew has medium brown-gray hair that kind of waves back over the top of his head, and his nose and teeth are just your ordinary sniffer and chompers. It's his eyes that are unusual. They're speckled. I think they're brown to begin with, but they've got so many green and blue and yellow spots in them that it's hard to tell. And when you look at them, you realize that everything else about Father Mayhew may seem ordinary, but his eyes are definitely complicated.

I first met him about two weeks after my mother dumped me at Grams' so she could run off to Hollywood and become a movie star. Grams figured that she finally had her chance and decided to have me baptized, so she hauled me to St. Mary's, and after a long meeting with Father Mayhew, well, there I was at the altar, getting doused with holy water while Grams sprinkled the ground with tears.

It didn't mean a whole lot to me, but I knew it was important to Grams. Funny thing is, after I got splashed with holy water, St. Mary's felt kind of like home. Father Mayhew started saying, "Good afternoon, Samantha," when he'd see me walking by, and when he'd ask me, "How are you, lass?" his complicated eyes would twinkle a bit, like he really wanted to know.

So when Grams talked to Father Mayhew about having me serve my twenty hours of detention at St. Mary's, he was very sympathetic and seemed glad to have an extra hand helping out.

When I reported to Father Mayhew's office for my first day, I saw a bucket of white paint, a roller, and a stack of rags on the floor, and Father Mayhew, removing pictures from the wall behind his desk. "Good afternoon, Samantha," he says, "I thought painting might be good penance." He leans an oil painting of the pope in front of one of Jesus on the cross. "Sort of a cleansing process, eh, lass?"

Then he removes a painting of cows grazing near missionaries hoeing a field. I jump back a little, because behind it is a wall safe. He laughs at my expression. "We have to have some place to keep our collections, don't we?"

I nod, but it still seems kind of strange, having that safe appear from behind cows grazing and missionaries hoeing.

"Now, take your time, lass. I only get 'round to this every ten years or so, so she'll need at least two coats." He whistles through his teeth and says, "Here, Gregory...Come on out, lad. She's all right."

Out from under his desk comes a dog. And he's not the kind of dog you'd ordinarily do a double take for. He's just a Welsh terrier—fairly small with wiry brown and black fur, and ears that kind of flip forward at the tips. But I *do* look at him twice because he's got a carrot in his mouth. A nice slobbery, droopy old carrot.

I look up at Father Mayhew to see if he knows his dog's hauling around vegetables, but he knows, all right. He laughs. "He's a taste for carotene, I'm afraid. Can't seem to break him of it." Then he ruffles Gregory's ears and says, "There are worse habits, I suppose."

Father Mayhew goes over to open up a window, and I kneel down and say, "Hi, boy!" to his dog.

Gregory wags his way over to me, panting and smiling right through his carrot. I laugh and scratch his chest, and then Father Mayhew turns from the window. For a moment he just stares, and then he says, "Well, I'll be."

I say, "What?" and stand up, because his eyes are looking extra complicated.

He shakes his head. "Gregory is not what you'd call a

social animal. The nuns are scared to death of him. Not that he's given them any real reason, mind you, but he does tend to growl at strangers."

He whistles for Gregory to follow him and says over his shoulder, "I'll be back in a bit to check on you. If you need anything, I'll be next door at the parish hall. Just come down."

I get busy rolling paint, and pretty soon I'm humming to myself because sprucing up Father Mayhew's office doesn't feel like detention at all. It's almost fun. And I'm getting the knack of rolling way up the wall without splattering myself in the face or bumping into the ceiling, and I'm stretching out with a really loaded roller when I hear, "Glory be! What a *fine* job you're doing!"

Well, there goes the roller, *bump,* right into the ceiling, and while I'm thinking Rats! because now there's a big white blotch on the ceiling, *splat!* I catch a drop of paint, right on my forehead.

So while I'm wiping paint off my face and out of my hair, I look over my shoulder and what I see taking up the whole doorway is a nun. A big, loud nun. She's grinning from ear to ear, and between her front teeth is a gap the size of a Popsicle stick. She says, "Child, you are *dripping,*" and then rushes in to save me from raining paint all over the office.

She gets the roller away from me, then grabs a rag and wipes my hands and face like I'm a little kid. "There now, that's better," she says, then flashes her gap again. "I'm Sister Bernice—or Sister Bernie—whatever you prefer. Who might you be?"

I smile back at her. "Hi. I'm Samantha Keyes—or Sammy—whatever *you* prefer."

She throws her head back and laughs, then sticks her hand out. "Nice to make your acquaintance, Sammy." And as she's pumping my hand up and down, she says, "I'm with the Sisters of Mercy. Father Mayhew's expecting us. We were told we could find him here...?"

What I really want to ask is, The Sisters of *what*? but instead I say, "He said he'd be at the parish hall." And I'm about to tell her how to get there when two other nuns appear in the doorway.

Now, no one has to tell me these nuns are with Sister Bernice. They're wearing black habits, too, which is what you might expect *all* nuns to wear, but they don't. Sister Josephine and Sister Mary Margaret never wear habits. They dress in gray skirts, simple white blouses, and sensible shoes—not as sensible as high-tops, but definitely sensible. And even though they don't wear habits, Sister Josephine and Sister Mary Margaret are still very nun-like. You just can't tell from three blocks away that they're nuns like you can with the ones that *do* wear habits.

Anyhow, I guess I was staring, because Sister Bernice follows my gaze and says, "Mercy me, that was fast, Sisters! Did you find a good spot?"

The tall one with red bangs says, "An excellent spot, right by the parish hall." She smiles at me. "And who have we here?"

Bernie puts an arm around me. "An angel—nothing less! This sweet thing was busy rolling over the sins of the past, bringing new life and spirit into the chambers of the holy."

The other two kind of look at me and smile, and I'm not real sure they know what Sister Bernice is talking about so I say, "I was painting Father Mayhew's office...?"

They say, "Of course you were, dear," and "After all these years we've come to understand Sister's way with words." The taller one puts out her hand and says, "I'm Sister Abigail, and this is Sister Clarice. It's nice to be with you in God's service."

Now, I'm not about to break it to them that their little angel was painting holy walls so she could work off some junior high detention time. I just shake hands and say, "It's nice to meet you."

Sister Bernice says to the other two, "So you found a spot over by the parish hall? Sammy here tells me that's where Father Mayhew can be found. Shall we continue our pilgrimage and make his acquaintance?"

So off they go, their habits shushing through the church, and I get back to covering up the sins of the past.

And I'm just finishing the first coat when Sister Josephine comes hobbling into the office. She asks, "Where's Father Mayhew?" then peeks under the desk and mumbles, "Hope he took that overgrown rabbit with him."

I put my roller down. "He left a little while ago—said he'd be over at the parish hall."

Sister Josephine is old. She's hunched over and walks with a cane—a thick black cane with a lot of nicks and scuffs on it. Some of the kids at school used to go to St. Mary's School when they were little and they say that the one thing they remember about third grade is Sister Josephine's cane. She'd pound it on the floor to get them to be quiet, she'd slap it against the chalkboard to get their attention, but mostly what they remember is that she'd whack it against their shins if she caught them lying or cheating.

Anyhow, she's standing there, hunched over, and all of a sudden her cane starts shaking. I'm not talking about a little quiver, either. That cane's got a serious wobble to it. And at first I think she's going to faint or have a stroke or something, but then I realize that this is one mad nun.

So I ask, "What's wrong?"

She points her cane at the wall like a pistol. "This is how it *always* goes. We ask and ask and ask for something and before you know it, *he* gets what we've been asking for!"

I don't know exactly what she's talking about, but before she starts firing that cane around I say, "Did *you* need some painting done, too?"

Down comes the cane, *whack*, onto the floor. "Our entire house needs paint, inside and out! Sister Mary Margaret and I have been telling him that for years. He always says there's no money for it, and here he is, having his office painted *again*."

I should've just stood there nodding or something, but instead I blurt, "I'm just doing this one wall. Father Mayhew said it hasn't been done in ten years."

"Ten years! I think it was just last year Christmas he had this wall painted." She takes a deep breath, then mumbles, "One of these days…" and then hobbles out.

I watch her go, and then get busy on the second coat,

wondering just how black and blue Father Mayhew's shins are.

It didn't take long to paint the wall again, and as I'm wiping up the last drips, Father Mayhew walks in with Gregory trotting along behind.

His shins don't seem to be bothering him at all, and he's in a great mood. "Ah, beautiful job, lass," he says, then winks a complicated eye at me. "A clean slate feels good, doesn't it?"

I know he's talking about more than just the color of his wall, so I nod and get busy closing up the can and wrapping up the roller. "Did Sister Josephine find you?"

He smiles. "That she did." Then he raises a brow and says, "Ah, the paint. That's what's upset her," and I can tell that Josephine waved that cane all around Father Mayhew, but never actually fired off about the paint.

So I say, "You want me to do some painting at their house tomorrow?"

"Hmm...That's sweet of you, lass, but no. It's across town, and besides, there's a lot of sanding needs to be done. It's really a job for a professional, I'm afraid."

"Did those other nuns find you?"

"Ah, the Sisters of Mercy. That they did." He winks and says, "Perhaps we'll have the money for some professional painting after our guests' fundraiser."

"So that's why they're here?"

"That's the reason. They've come to help out with the Thanksgiving food drive, but it looks like they'll be doing much more than that." He goes over to his filing cabinet, takes a carrot out of the top drawer, and says, "That Sis-

10

ter Bernice is a fountain of ideas. I've never met anyone quite like her." He gives Gregory the new carrot, then smiles at me and says, "Run along now, lass. Tomorrow I'll have you clean the windows in the church, if you don't mind?"

I say, "Sounds fine," and head for home.

And the next day there's Father Mayhew, waiting for me, Windex in hand. He gets me a ladder and shows me the stained-glass windows he wants washed, and then says, "Now, if someone comes in to worship, I want you to move to the back of the church and just wait. It may take you a few days to do all the windows, but that's all right. It's better than interfering in someone's time with God."

So I take my rags and Windex and for a long time it's just me and the windows. Then a lady in a shawl comes in, so I wait. And wait and wait. And when she leaves, a man and a woman come in and just kind of sit in the back and cry for a while. So I wait and wait some more, feeling bad that they're sitting there crying.

When they left, I got back to work again, and I guess I was concentrating on buffing glass because I didn't even notice there was anyone else in the church until I got off the ladder and stood back to look at the window.

She was on her way out of the church before I could get a very good look at her, but what I could see was that she was thin, had a brown ponytail, and was about my age. Now, kids don't usually come to church in the middle of the afternoon on a school day—they're too busy running around town trying to put together enough sins to make going to church on Sunday worthwhile. So her just being

11

there was enough to make me do a double take, but it was her shoes that made me want to go up to her and say, "Hi!"

She was wearing high-tops. Like mine, only older. And I was about to chase after her, only just then Father Mayhew comes through the side door and says, "Samantha, I want to see you. Right now! In my office!" and I could tell from the way his voice was booming through the church that something was wrong.

Very wrong.

TWO

I followed him, all right. Straight back to his office. And when he sits down behind his desk and stares at me, I stand in front of it and ask, "What happened? What's wrong?"

He swivels in his chair for a minute while his fingers push back and forth against each other. Then he takes a deep breath and says, "As I'm sure you know, we religious take a vow of poverty. The Church provides us with food and shelter and a modest living allowance, but by and large, we own very little. Very few things that I have do I consider to be *mine*. Do you understand this, Samantha?"

This priest sitting behind the desk may have looked like Father Mayhew, but he sure didn't *sound* like him. I just gulped and said, "Yes, sir."

He takes another deep breath like he's counting to ten. "One of my few earthly treasures is my papal cross." He's quiet for a long time, pushing his fingers up and down. Then he says, "It was given to me by my father when I was ordained. He has since passed on, and it can never be replaced." He looks straight at me. "Samantha, I implore you—give it back. There'll be no repercussions—just, please, return it."

Now I *think* I know what cross he's talking about. Whenever Father Mayhew gives a service, he wears this ivory cross on a knotted rope of ivory beads. It's not a plain cross or one with Jesus on it like you're used to seeing. It's got one big cross bar with two smaller ones above it—like the top of a power-line pole. So I ask, "Your ivory cross?"

His fingers freeze. "Please, lass, give it back."

"But Father Mayhew, I didn't steal your cross!"

"Samantha, please. It's very important to me."

"I don't have it!"

"Samantha…"

"Really, I don't!"

He shoots out of his chair. "Well, if you insist on denying it, then perhaps it'd be best if you spent your time with Sister Josephine over at the soup kitchen." He comes from behind his desk, and you can tell from the way he's moving that he wants me *out* of there.

I say, "But…" but he refuses to listen, and the next thing you know I've been thrown out of church.

I stood on the walkway, staring at St. Mary's front door, not quite believing what had just happened. Why did he think *I'd* stolen his cross? Just because I'd broken some rules at school didn't make me a thief! But I could tell that this new Father Mayhew was not someone to argue with, so after a few minutes of standing around fuming, I headed over to the soup kitchen.

The soup kitchen doesn't serve soup. Not that I've ever seen, anyway. It mostly serves sandwiches or just prepackaged food. I'd never actually been inside the soup kitchen, but I'd watched people waiting for it to open or eating on the benches outside.

14

Some strange people hang out at the soup kitchen. It's next to the Salvation Army, and right between them is this grassy area where people spend the day passing cigarettes around, checking out bandannas on other guys' dogs, or rocking strollers back and forth, trying to keep their babies from crying.

And whenever I walk by, I wonder how the people got there. Do they have homes? Do they sleep in the bushes? What do they do when it rains? Grams calls them bums and usually I do, too, and the ones who hang out in the grass all day asking you for money when you walk by, well, I think they are.

But then I'll see a really old man standing in line and wonder how he wound up at the soup kitchen. Did he start out sharing cigarettes and checking out bandannas? Or did he go out for a walk one day and forget how to get home.

I've thought about following them to see where they go at night, but according to Marissa and Dot, half of them really *do* have homes and the other half camp out under the Stowell Road overpass.

Anyhow, there I am, knocking on the front door of the soup kitchen while all the bums in town are checking me out. Finally, someone opens the door and says, "We're not open for another half hour."

Well, it's Brother Phil, and if you knew Brother Phil, you'd know why I had to stick my foot in the door. Phil is kind of, well, dense. He's got a round face and a round belly, and a very round head. A very *dense* round head. Normally, you don't think about a person's head, but with

15

Brother Phil you can't help it. He's mostly bald, only I don't think he's quite admitted that to himself yet. He plasters what hair he has left from one side of his head clear over the top to the other side. And since Brother Phil's got such a round head, no matter what he does, there's always a patch where his scalp shines through like a flashlight in a bat cave.

Brother Phil's not the kind of guy you try to explain things to. He doesn't *listen* real well. He has his own ideas about things, and getting him to change his mind is like opening a gate that's swelled shut in the rain.

So before Brother Phil can slam the door in my face, I stick my high-top in and say, "Father Mayhew sent me over."

He says, "Fine, but we won't be serving for another half hour," while he's pushing on the door trying to figure out why it won't close.

"Brother Phil, he sent me over to help, not to eat!"

He just stares at me. Then one of his eyes twitches a few times and he asks, "You're here to *help*?"

I let myself in. "That's right."

Sitting at a table in the kitchen are Sister Josephine and Sister Mary Margaret, and they're hovering over a map. Sister Josephine looks up and then scrambles out of her chair. "What are you doing here?" she asks, like I've caught her having a swig of holy water.

Before I can answer, she turns to Brother Phil and says, "What's going on?"

"Mayhew sent her over. To help, I guess."

I just stand there like an idiot, wishing I was back

scrubbing purple glass, when Sister Mary Margaret stands up and says, "Well that's wonderful! We can always use an extra hand." She points to the map and says, "Sister and I were just planning our vacation—"

Brother Phil cuts in, saying, "I don't know why you have to plan it out. You go to Las Vegas every year. And you take the bus!"

Sister Josephine picks up her cane, kind of cocking it in case Brother Phil gets even farther out of line. "Last year, if you recall, the bus broke down and we had to wait five hours in the middle of the desert for someone to repair it. If we'd had a map, maybe we could've done something about it."

Brother Phil shakes his head. "Like *what*?"

Sister Mary Margaret shrugs and says, "Who knows, Philip...maybe hitchhike."

So I'm trying to picture the two of them on the side of the road with their thumbs out, when Mary Margaret folds the map up real neat and says, "Regardless, it's our little adventure and we're enjoying it." She turns to me. "What's your name again, dear?"

"Sammy. Sammy Keyes."

She smiles. "That's right. You come Sundays with your grandmother, don't you?"

I give her a little nod.

"Not every Sunday, though."

Well, that's a little unnerving, let me tell you. I mean *lots* of people go to St. Mary's on Sundays. How could she possibly notice if I'm not there?

Her eyes give me a quick reprimand. Then she smiles

17

and says, "So, have you ever worked in a relief kitchen before?"

"No, Sister."

"It's not hard. You'll find most of the people are very nice. If any of them give you a lick of trouble, just point them out to one of us and we'll take care of it." She checks her watch and says, "It looks like we'd better set up. It's almost time."

So we wash up, and then Brother Phil starts hauling trays of sandwiches out of the refrigerator while the Sisters bring out cartons of punch and milk. When the food's all set up, Mary Margaret says, "Each person gets one sandwich, two cookies, a bag of chips, and something to drink. If they have children, insist on the milk."

Sister Josephine says, "And if they ask for more, tell them no. We're not here to feed their dogs, no matter what some of them think!" Then she says to Phil, "Let 'em in," and disappears.

The way the soup kitchen is set up to serve people is, there's a ramp to the door where they come in, there's a table where they pick up their plate of food, and there's a door with an EXIT sign where they go out.

When Brother Phil opens the door, the first person to come in is a woman pushing a baby in a stroller. I say, "Hi," to her and she mumbles, "Bueno." I put together a plate for her with an extra milk and say, "There you go," but she doesn't even look at me. She just takes the food and leaves.

I tried being friendly to the next couple of people who came in, but it seemed to make them uncomfortable, so I just started handing out food, asking, "Punch or milk?"

and tried to keep the line moving. And before you know it I'm on autopilot, thinking about Father Mayhew and his cross, and what I can do to convince him that I didn't steal it.

Then this man with tattoos shows up. He's got blue snakes wrapping up his arms and clear around his neck, and he points to the sandwiches and says, "Let me have another."

I say, "Sorry. We're only supposed to give out one apiece," so he reaches over and *takes* one, then shows me all his rotten teeth like, Oh yeah? Well come and get it!

Phil yells, "Hey! Put it back!" but the guy just snarls, then spits on the floor and leaves.

That wound Brother Phil up, all right. I thought he was going to spring his little round body right over the food table and chase after him, but what he did instead was sputter around in circles for a minute, then holler, "Move back, move back! Quit crowding!" to the people coming in the door.

After that, I quit brooding about Father Mayhew and started paying more attention to what I was doing. And when this man comes through pushing a stroller with a blanket draped over it and whispers, "I'd like some food for my kid, too," something about it didn't seem quite right. And before I could stop myself, I reached over and pulled the blanket back. And what do I see? A jacket stuffed with clothes.

He yanks the blanket back and says, "Keep your hands off my stuff, you nosy brat!" Then he tries to cover up by saying, "I got a kid—he's just asleep outside."

I say, "Right," and try to help the next person. But he doesn't leave. He stands there and says, "Hand it over!"

Out of nowhere pops Sister Mary Margaret. She says, "Young man, the police station is two blocks away. If I hear another peep out of you, I'm going to pick up the phone and call. I suggest you take your sandwich and enjoy what's left of the sunshine."

He looks at her like a puppy that's nipped his own tail, and then hurries out the door.

So there I am, passing out food, thinking about what's just happened, when all of a sudden I'm standing face to face with this *girl*. She's my size and her hair's back in a ponytail, just like mine, and she's not there with her mom or dad—she's all by herself. And I'm standing there, holding out a plate to her, not quite wanting to let go of it when it hits me that she's the girl I saw at St. Mary's.

I look under the table and, sure enough, she's wearing high-tops. I smile at her and say, "Hi!" but all she does is look at me kind of suspiciously. Then she takes the food and leaves.

Now you have to understand—it's not every day I say hi to someone like I want to be friends with them. I mean, I've got Marissa and Dot, and other than that I don't need any friends. People I know with lots of friends don't seem to have any real friends. It's like doubling the recipe when you've only got half the sugar—you wind up with a lot of cupcakes, but they're not very sweet.

But there I was, being friendly to a perfect stranger, wishing she'd come back so I could talk to her and find out some important stuff—like her name and where she gets her high-tops.

And what in the world she's doing, getting her dinner at the soup kitchen.

THREE

Attending William Rose Junior High School is not my idea of a pleasure cruise. It's more like camping out in the Rocky Mountains without a jacket—if the cold doesn't get you, the mosquitoes will, and the only thing to do is keep moving around so you're not an easy target.

School itself is all right. It's even interesting sometimes if you've got the right teachers. It's all the other stuff that makes it a pain. Stuff like gossip and cliques and Heather Acosta. Especially Heather Acosta.

For a little while there I thought Heather was going to leave me alone. She'd walk right by me without so much as a snide word, which is something Heather could normally never do. Maybe her psychiatrist told her to act like that. Who knows? All I know is that it didn't take long for her to start giving me the Evil Eye again.

I've been trying to ignore her. I mean, I have her in homeroom and science, but we've been moved way across the room from each other, so if those were the only times I saw her, I could pretty much just avoid her.

Trouble is, she's playing intramural softball and so am I. She's on the team that was just ranked number one in the whole school and guess who's on the team ranked right beneath her. We've never been beaten and *they've* never been beaten, but somehow they're number one and we're number two.

And starting next week, it's us against them in a best-out-of-three playoff for who gets to represent the school at the Junior Sluggers' Cup Tournament, so Heather's been sharpening her claws.

I'd made it through homeroom without so much as a twitch of the Evil Eye from Heather, but at lunch she walks by our table with some of her friends and says, "You losers are going to bite the dust on Monday."

I just ignore her, but Dot says, "Are you telling us Mr. Vince got a new shortstop?"

We all laugh and slap hands, but Heather doesn't think there's too much funny about that. She comes back a few steps. "You guys think you're so smart..."

I smile at her. "No, Heather—you just make us look that way."

It takes her a second, but pretty soon her face is as red as her hair and it takes both Tenille Toolee and Monet Jarlsberg to haul her away saying stuff like, "Take it easy, Heather," and "Don't let her get to you."

That put a grin on my face for the rest of the day.

Now the fact that Heather Acosta *wants* to play softball tells you something about Santa Martina. In this town if you don't play softball, you might as well not be alive. It's a *huge* deal. Teams play year round, rain or shine. Grams says the community would sooner cancel Christmas than a softball game, and I think she's right. People are nuts for it. And at our level, winning the Junior Sluggers' Cup is like winning the Super Bowl.

So all of us keep a pretty good eye on each other. Watching other players teaches you a lot about them, which comes in really handy if you play with them. Or against them. And I hate to admit it, but Heather really is a pretty good shortstop, which is how she made it on a team of mostly eighth graders. I don't know how in the world Tenille made the cut. She plays right field and mostly just puts her glove up and prays when a ball comes her way. What that backstabbing little spy Monet's doing on second base is easy to figure out—she's blackmailed someone into giving her that position. Maybe even Mr. Vince.

Mr. Vince teaches eighth-grade history, but he lives to coach and his team usually wins. So I guess I should want to be on his team, but really, he gives me the creeps. It's one thing that he's got the IQ of an aphid and talks like he's got a mouth full of sawdust, but what makes me want to puke is how he's always joking around with the eighth-grade girls and offering to buy them sodas. And when it comes to softball, he thinks he's the God of Strategy. Please.

Anyway, Heather's on his team, which would be reason enough for me to be glad to be on the other team. But I also really like our coach. Ms. Rothhammer's tough but she's smart and she's fair. She spends part of the day teaching P.E. and the other part teaching eighth-grade biology. I've heard that she can pith and dissect a frog in fifteen seconds, and that you don't want to be anywhere *near* her while she's whipping a scalpel around.

At first the eighth graders grumbled a lot about Dot,

Marissa, and me being on their team because we're just lowly seventh graders. But they figured out in a hurry that all grumbling got them was laps and push-ups, so now they don't actually *say* anything about us being on their team—they just don't include us. And I'm sure a lot of them think they'd be ranked number one instead of number two if only some eighth graders could magically take our place.

They're wrong, and the reason they're wrong is Marissa. If it weren't for her, we wouldn't have made it nearly as far as we have. Marissa may sometimes act kind of skittery, but when she gets on the mound, she turns into a pitching machine. She's cool and calm and can put the ball over the plate every time, any way she wants. You can practically see her shut everything out. Everything but the strike zone and her catcher, that is.

And that's where I come in. Being catcher is not exactly the position most people want when they try out for a softball team. Pitcher, shortstop, second base, first base—those are popular. But catcher? It's dusty and sweaty and hard on the legs. But ever since the day I found a catcher's mitt in Grams' closet, I've *wanted* to play catcher.

What Grams was doing with a catcher's mitt in her closet was something I sure couldn't figure out, so as soon as our nosy neighbor Mrs. Graybill was gone and I could come up for air, I popped out and asked Grams, "Where'd you get this?"

She just stares. First at the mitt, then at me. Then she takes her glasses off, huffs and buffs them some, and says, "I fished it out of the garbage."

"You *what?* Why?"

Grams sits down on the edge of the bed and sighs. "It belonged to your mother."

It was my turn to stare. "Lady Lana played *softball?*" I mean, my mother thinks it's strenuous to vacuum, and I couldn't exactly see her in the middle of a dust bowl with face gear on, squatting to catch balls.

Grams takes a deep breath. "Not exactly."

"Well, then, what was she doing with a catcher's mitt?" Silence.

"Grams!"

She sighs. "It was your father's."

That made me a little wobbly around the knees, and the next thing you know I'm sliding down the closet door, saying, "My *father?*" because my father is someone Grams will not talk about. Doesn't think it's her place.

Lady Lana doesn't like to talk about him either, except to say that he was a mistake she wished she'd never made. I asked her once if he knew about me. All she said was, "No." I asked if she had a picture of him. All she said was, "No." Then, when I asked if she knew where he was, she said, "No, and we're not going to discuss this anymore until you're older." I tried telling her I was plenty old enough, but she got up and walked out of the room.

I sat there feeling like a kid who'd tried all year to be good and then found a chunk of cement in her Christmas stocking. And a few months later, when Lady Lana dumped me at Grams', well, I couldn't help feeling that my father wasn't the biggest mistake my mother had ever made—I was.

So when Grams told me that the catcher's mitt belonged to my father, I just sat there on the floor staring at it. I turned it over and over. I pulled on the knots. I put my hand inside it and then buried my face in it until all I could smell was leather and dust. And when I finally came up for air, I knew that the next time I played softball I'd play catcher—and I'd do it with my dad's mitt.

And you may think this is kind of stupid, but I carry it with me all the time. Mostly it's in my backpack smashed between my books, but I like knowing it's there. Some kids carry pictures of their family in their wallets. You should see Dot's! She's got two brothers and two sisters and a billion cousins. She's got a whole *album* of snapshots in her wallet. Me, I've got my mitt. And even though it's not a photograph or a letter or even a present from him, it's a little piece of my dad. A piece that's all mine.

Turns out I'm a *good* catcher. Of course, Marissa had something to do with that—last summer she spent a lot of time coaching me. But I am pretty good, and with Marissa pitching, I look great.

I'm also fast. Not quite as fast as Dot, but no one is. You should see her run the bases or chase down balls—that girl *flies*. She can be on third, dive for a ball down the line, get up and throw to first, and be back in position before the umpire's made the call. Even Ms. Rothhammer says she's never seen anyone as fast as Dot, and that's quite a compliment coming from ol' Speedy Scalpel.

Anyway, the eighth graders may not want us to be on their team, but we've come this far in the tournament and there's no getting rid of us now. And even with their attitude and Heather's little threat of dust consumption, it seemed like nothing could shake our good mood.

On the walk home from school, Dot's making jokes and busting us up with commentary like, "And now it's Heather Acosta's turn at bat. The pitch is good and it's a...line drive past third. The left fielder bobbles the ball...but wait! What's this? Acosta is dragging the bat along with her...they've called her out! Was that sheer excitement on her part or...wait! It seems that...yes...it appears that her *fingernails* have embedded themselves into the bat. What's that, Don? You think they're *through* the bat? Is that possible? Ladies and gentlemen, this is sensational! Acosta is pulling the bat with all her might but cannot seem to release herself! Her coach is now helping her, and *he* doesn't seem to be able to get those claws out of that bat. They're taking her off the field now, and they're calling for shears. Looks like they'll need *pruning* shears on those babies!"

By now I'm laughing so hard that when we get to the mall there's no way I want to just say "Bye" and head for St. Mary's. So when Marissa asks, "Do you have time for a Juicers?" I say, "You bet!" and follow her and Dot into the mall.

So the three of us are stepping out of the elevator at the mall, still laughing, when who do I see? The Sisters of Mercy.

Now, they're not out praying or converting. They're shopping, and I mean *shopping*. Bernice has about ten bags hanging from her arms, and Abigail and Clarice are saddled up pretty good, too.

I say, "Hey, you guys, look! Over at the Braddock's window. Those are the nuns I was telling you about!"

Dot says, "*Those* are the Sisters of Mercy?"

I laugh. "Yeah! They're a riot. Want to meet them?"

So off we go, only before we get to Braddock's, the Sisters pop inside. So we stand outside, watching and waiting. Sister Bernice drops all her packages in a corner and runs around the store flicking through dress racks, feeling scarves, holding things up for the other two to see. Sister Abigail looks around, but she doesn't touch much and spends more time checking out what Sister Clarice is holding up than anything else. And even though they're in there for quite a while, we don't mind. I mean, watching nuns shop is funny—kind of like it'd be to see Father Mayhew get up and karaoke.

When they get done combing through the store, Bernice shoves a new bag on her arm and practically knocks me over as she comes out the door.

At first she doesn't recognize me, but when I say, "Hi, Sister Bernice!" she flashes her gap and says, "Mercy me! If it isn't our new friend Sammy." Then she says, "Look, Sisters! Sammy's caught us doing our Christmas shopping."

Clarice and Abigail say hello, and I say, "These are my friends, Marissa and Dot."

Bernice throws her head back and laughs, then shakes Dot's hand and says, "Dot. What a wonderful way to thank God for making you special. That's a name I shan't forget."

When most people first meet Dot, they try real hard not to stare. She's got a beauty mark on one of her cheeks and at first, well, that's all you really notice. It's not gross—

it's just a perfect circle that looks like a small splat of paint. But after you've known Dot awhile, you don't even really see the dot anymore. You just see Dot.

Bernice breaks her eyes away from Dot's dot and says, "Well, we'd better move along. I still have nieces and nephews to buy for, and oh, yes! Aunt Isabelle. Don't let me forget Aunt Isabelle!"

As they walk away, Dot laughs and says, "Wow."

We get drinks at Juicers, and when we're about done, Marissa asks, "What are you guys doing tomorrow? Do you want to get together and practice for Monday?"

I say, "Sure," and so does Dot because it's easy to see that Marissa's worried about getting slaughtered on Monday.

I ask, "At the park?"

"Cool. How about ten?"

Dot says, "Oh, I can't at ten! I've got to take Nibbles over to the Pup Parlor for a dip at ten."

Marissa and I look at each other and then at Dot. "A *dip*?"

Dot blushes a little and whispers, "He's got fleas."

I say, "Well, why don't we all just meet over at the Pup Parlor at ten, then walk over to the park and practice until Nibbles is ready?"

Everyone thinks that's a good idea, so I say, "I've got to get over to St. Mary's. See you tomorrow!"

Now, I've been trying to avoid thinking about it all day, telling myself that for once I just need to keep *out* of it, but as I'm heading over to the soup kitchen, I know that before I spend the rest of the afternoon dodging Sister Josephine's cane, there's somewhere else I've *got* to go.

FOUR

Gregory saw me first. He wiggled out from under the desk and laid what was left of his carrot at my feet. I laughed and scratched his chest and whispered, "No thanks, boy."

Father Mayhew was standing over by the window with his hands behind his back, looking outside. At first I thought he might be having a word with God so I tried to be quiet, whispering, "No, boy, no!" when Gregory nosed his carrot stump in my direction.

But after a little while I could tell that he was just thinking. And since I was getting tired of being chased around by a carrot, I cleared my throat and said, "Excuse me...Father Mayhew?"

He jumped a bit and then wiped his eyes, and when he realized it was me, he put on a stern face and walked to his desk. "What is it, Samantha?"

Well, all of a sudden I can't find any words. I mean, here he is, sitting behind his big desk, pretending to be in complete control, but his complicated eyes are red around the edges and it's easy to see that he's been crying. I whisper, "I was hoping you'd found your cross...?"

"Noooo." He blows his nose and sighs. "It wasn't misplaced, lass, it was taken."

He was still looking pretty stony, but he *had* said lass, so

31

I inched into his office and sat in a chair against the wall. "Father Mayhew, I swear, I didn't take your cross. I don't know who did, but it wasn't me. Was it in this office the day I painted? Is that why you think I took it?"

He studies me a minute. "It was in the sacristy." Then he points to a door at the back of his office and says, "Right through there. I left it open because I thought it would help with the ventilation while you were painting."

Now the whole time Father Mayhew's talking, his dog's inching over to me with that carrot stump in his mouth. Finally, he just makes a break for it. He comes over, dumps his slobbery carrot in my lap and then sits next to me, grinning from ear to ear. He's acting like he wants me to play carrot catch, but I don't feel like tossing a slimy orange stump around. I put it on the floor next to me and ask Father Mayhew, "Is that the only door to the sacristy?"

He says, "No, there's a door in the hallway," but what he's concentrating on is Gregory picking the carrot up and putting it back in my lap.

I say, "Was it locked? I mean, did someone have to come through your office to take the cross?" and really, I'm trying hard to ignore how Gregory's nudging that carrot around my lap, but it's getting a little out of hand.

He says, "What? Oh. No. It wasn't locked, but it *was* closed."

"But anybody could've walked in if they'd wanted to?"

By now little Gregory has decided my lap is also a good place for his front paws, and before I can stop him, he's on my lap and in my face, panting away, huffing carrot breath all over me.

Father Mayhew's complicated eyes are looking very confused, let me tell you. He says, "Off, lad! Off!" so Gregory jumps down, but he doesn't go far. He rests his nose on my knee and keeps one eye on me, and one on that carrot, which is still in my lap.

Father Mayhew mumbles, "I suppose so. But that's the only thing missing. Why would someone walk in, steal my cross, and leave? There are things far more valuable in the sacristy."

"Was it where you always keep it when you're not wearing it?"

"I had it ready with my vestments for a service last night. Right around the hanger."

"So anyone who knows you would know that if you're not wearing it, your cross is probably hanging with your robe in that room?"

He sits up a little. "You're implying that one of the *religious* took it?"

I sneak the carrot stump onto the floor again and say, "I don't know—maybe a janitor? A cleaning lady? Who goes in there?"

While he's thinking about this, Gregory picks up the carrot, puts it back in my lap, then lets out a growl. A long, low growl.

I jump back a little, and then Sister Josephine walks in. And Gregory keeps right on growling as he backs himself completely under Father Mayhew's desk.

Father Mayhew coos, "Easy, lad, easy," then asks, "Yes, Sister? What is it?"

Now, I don't think Josephine noticed I was there,

because the door was sort of blocking her view. She thumps the floor with her cane and says, "That is the rudest bunch of ingrates I have ever met. In all my years in the church I have never had to tolerate such brazen, intrusive, unappreciative creatures!" Then she mutters, "They may as well be Baptists."

Father Mayhew conjures up a cough. "Now, now, Sister. Calm down. You may not approve of their personalities, but they come highly recommended and I have full confidence they'll bring out community goodwill." He leans back in his chair and makes a little fingertip tent with his hands. "Would you like to tell me what happened?"

Josephine crosses her arms so the crook of her cane is hooked on her shoulder like a giant bird claw. "You want to know what happened? I'll tell you what happened. We went through with your suggestion to have them over for lunch. Sister and I worked all morning preparing lamb stroganoff. They arrived forty minutes late with not so much as an I'm sorry. They just whisked in empty-handed and expected to be served. And then, *then*...they didn't like the stroganoff! Abigail is allergic to mushrooms, Clarice doesn't eat lamb, and Bernice—*Bernice* picked out the lamb and left the noodles." She thumps her cane back on the floor. "Would you kindly tell me how such a large woman can be a picky eater?"

Just then, Gregory turns up the volume. Way up. And he's growling so loud that Josephine slams her cane right by his nose and hisses, "Stop that, you oversized rodent!"

Father Mayhew says, "Quiet, lad!" And he's about to

scold Josephine, too, when he notices Sister Bernice standing in the doorway.

Sister Josephine sees her picky eater standing there and freezes. But Bernie comes in with a bright smile and says, "Sister! Father! Sammy! Lordy-be, it's Grand Central in here! Father, you need to ask the Mighty One for a bigger office!" Then she hears Gregory growling away under the desk. She bends down and says, "Now, now, pup. Sister Bernie's not gonna hurt ya. Come on out and give her a kiss!"

Gregory stays put, but he does quiet down a bit, and when Father Mayhew says to Josephine, "Perhaps we can finish our discussion later?" Josephine just scowls and hobbles out the door.

Bernie looks over her shoulder. "Is something troubling Sister?"

Father Mayhew shakes his head and says, "Not to worry. Now, what is it I can help you with?"

"A few things, Father. First, last night someone tried to break into our motor home—"

Father Mayhew's eyebrows go popping up. "My word! Was anything taken?"

Bernice shakes her head and says, "No, we scared him off, praise God, but next time—who knows? And since I've seen quite a number of lost lambs roaming the neighborhood, I was hoping you wouldn't mind storing a valuable of mine in your safe." She motions to the missionaries and cows hanging on the wall. "I noticed it when Sammy here was toiling away."

Father Mayhew says, "Certainly. What is it you'd like me to keep for you?"

She pulls out a locket and dangles it by the chain as she hands it over to him. "My sister Sandra has entrusted me to deliver this to my niece Olivia. It's been passed down from mother to daughter for five generations, and if I failed in my mission I could never forgive myself."

Father Mayhew takes the locket, then lifts the cows and missionaries off their nail, and gets busy twirling the dial. I can't see exactly what he's doing because he's got his back to us, but I see his wall safe open, I see him put the locket inside, and I see him spin the dial when he shuts the safe. Then he replaces the painting and says, "You let me know when you need it back. If I'm not here...well, I will be. You just let me know."

Bernice's eyebrow arches up. "But if you're not, one of the Sisters can return it to me, can't they?"

Father Mayhew scratches behind his ear. "They have their own lockbox. If you're concerned, you can ask them to keep it for you."

Sister Bernice says, "I'm being silly. Of course you'll be here! We'll be continuing our mission after our final performance next Saturday—I know you won't be missing that!"

"Not for the world. I've a feeling it's going to be quite a show." He sits back behind his desk and eyes a manila envelope in her hand. "What else can I do for you, Sister?"

Bernice hands over the envelope and chuckles. "Continue to be even-tempered and patient." As Father Mayhew pulls out a pile of forms, she sighs and says, "It's quite a stack, I know, but in our work we have to be very careful to account for every penny. The government wants to know everything from A to Z about the people we've raised funds for, so you'll find some very tiresome questions in there. But we're in quite a stew by the end of the year if we don't have our paperwork in order." He flips through the forms as she says, "We're also in need of some names. Connections. We usually do a newspaper, radio, and television blitz and it's better to go in with an editor or station manager's name than it is to go in cold. I'll need a list of those, and any personal contacts you may have."

Now, this is not the Bernice I'm used to seeing. She's not laughing and talking in rhymes, or being buddy-buddy. She's business, all business. This woman knows how to put a fundraiser together, and heaven help anyone who moves too slow or tries to get in her way.

I think Father Mayhew was picking up on the same thing because he nods and says, "I'll have you a list by noon tomorrow. And I'll get these forms done tonight."

"I'll also need a mailing list and someone to help stuff envelopes." Bernice crinkles up one side of her face. "Sister Josephine and Sister Mary Margaret don't seem like the envelope-stuffing kind. Any suggestions?"

Well, anything's better than being Gregory's carrot caddie, so I say, "I could help...if that's all right with you, Father Mayhew?"

He studies me, then says, "Starting Monday. An hour with them, then an hour in the soup kitchen. How's that?"

"Sounds great!"

Sister Bernice flashes her gap at me and says, "Amen!" Then she notices the wall clock. "Lordy-be, it's getting late! And I've a million things to do yet." She waves and says, "Thank you, Father. We'll see you Monday, Sammy!" and then disappears.

The minute Bernice is gone, Gregory comes out from under the desk and retrieves his carrot. Only he doesn't go back under the desk, he lies down right next to me and starts gnawing.

Father Mayhew says, "Now, where were we?" but before I can answer, he looks at Gregory and shakes his head. "I've never seen him behave like this before. Ever. And the doubts I had about you, lass—they're gone. You have a good heart, that's easy to see, and I'm very sorry for the way I accused you yesterday. The cross is gone and I'm upset, but there's no sense in casting blame upon the innocent." Then he sighs. "I only wish I knew who stole it."

"What about the janitor?"

Father Mayhew shakes his head. "Not Enaldo. He's a good man. He's been with the church for twenty-five years."

"Who else comes through here? It has to be somebody that knows that's where you keep it. It's ivory, right? How valuable is it?"

Father Mayhew rubs his cheek. "I've never stopped to think of it in monetary terms. It's valuable to me for sentimental reasons. But it is very old and it *is* ivory.... I suppose you could get a pretty penny for it."

Now, my brain's telling me not to ask, but my mouth has other ideas. "Maybe someone took it to get back at you?"

He drills me with his complicated eyes. "Get *back* at me? Lass, what are you talking about?"

Now I'm feeling like a sparrow in a chimney—I can go up or I can go down, but either way, I'm going to be a mess by the time I'm out. I take a deep breath and decide to go up. "Uh…maybe some people have some resentments or something? You know, don't *like* you?"

He shakes his head. "They can always come talk to me. That's no reason to steal my cross!"

I nod kind of slowly. "Maybe they don't think talking's going to do them any good. Maybe they're just mad."

Now, *I* know I'm thinking about Sister Josephine, and *he* knows I'm thinking about Sister Josephine, but I'm not about to say it and neither is he. So we both sit there staring at each other like a couple of zombies. Finally, he looks down and says, "She wouldn't have done that. She may have a sharp tongue, but I know Sister Josephine to be an honorable woman."

He stands up and says, "I'm glad you came in, Samantha. You've given me a lot to think about, and once again, please accept my apology."

I say, "Thank you. I'm really sorry about your cross," and as I'm getting up to head over to the soup kitchen, Gregory jumps up, wagging his tail. I say, "Stay boy, stay!" and then zip out of there before ol' Carrot Killer can catch me.

And as I leave the church and pass along the tidy hedge surrounding the Virgin Mary, it strikes me that for a place that looks so calm and peaceful on the outside, St. Mary's is like a bubbling volcano on the inside.

And in the back of my brain I know—it won't be long before it blows.

FIVE

Brother Phil let me in through the back door of the soup kitchen and said, "They've decided they're driving."

I say, "Driving?" Then I see Josephine and Mary Margaret looking at a map and remember about their trip to Las Vegas.

"Yep. They're taking their sack of nickels and heading out."

Now, Josephine's not acting anything like she was back in Father Mayhew's office. She's laughing and rubbing her hands together and in general acting happy. And since I've never really seen her act like this before, I stop and whisper to Phil, "When are they leaving?"

Phil doesn't whisper back. I don't think he *can,* if you know what I mean. He's like an idling chain saw—even when he's not actually doing anything, he makes so much noise you want to cover your ears. He breathes loud, and talks loud, and even *walks* loud. Maybe it's because his feet are so big, I don't know, but they just seem to scuff and slap and bump a lot.

So when I ask him when the Sisters are leaving for Las Vegas, he practically yells, "Right after Thanksgiving," and then stubs his toe on the leg of a chair.

He hops around for a minute, then slams the chair back against the wall. "Who put that stupid thing here?"

Mary Margaret and Josephine look up and see me, then check the clock and say, "Good heavens, look at the time!"

While we're getting the food out, the nuns are talking about their trip, getting excited all over again about who they're going to stop and see, and what they're going to be able to do driving that they couldn't do on a bus.

Brother Phil, though, doesn't say a word. He just walks around with a great big frown on his face, idling. Sister Mary Margaret notices, and says, "Now Phil, don't take it so hard. You know you're needed here."

Phil shakes his head and mutters, "Seems I'm not needed anywhere..."

Josephine snaps, "Oh, don't start with that again, Phillip. It's getting tiresome. We all have our own calling. You may not have accepted yours yet, but the sooner you do, the happier you'll be."

Now, Mary Margaret doesn't like the way Josephine's treating Phil. She gives her a stern little look, then goes up to Phil and says, "Don't give up. It may take some time, but if you're meant to be ordained, Father'll see the light and help you."

Phil rolls his eyes. "It's never gonna happen. Last week he came right out and said I wasn't priest material."

Josephine's ears perk up. Then she shakes her head and mutters, "That man has some nerve...even if it's true." Then she starts winding herself up, saying, "I don't know where he—" but Sister Mary Margaret signals for her to cool it. Josephine eyes me and says, "Well, let's not just stand around. There's work to do!"

Serving the food went a lot better than it had the day before. One guy came in with his dog, which really set Josephine off, but other than that it was almost boring. And just when I thought we were all done serving, the girl I'd seen in the church comes running in, her backpack clinking as she moves. I smile at her and say, "Hi!" but she just gives me a quick nod, gets her food, and hurries out the exit.

Then I see Marissa and Dot peeking in all bug-eyed, looking like a couple of mice in a haunted house. I laugh and call, "Hi, guys!"

They come hurrying over and Marissa whispers, "Cool!" like she can't believe how lucky I am, having to serve a detention at the soup kitchen.

Dot says, "So this is it, huh?" Then she looks over her shoulder and whispers, "Who was that girl with the blue backpack? For a second there I thought it was you."

"I don't know. I've tried talking to her, but she just takes her food and leaves."

Marissa's eyes bug way out. "You're kidding! She's homeless? I thought maybe she was helping out, like you."

"I don't know if she's *homeless*—I've never seen her hanging around outside..." Then I get a bright idea. "Hey, you want to follow her?"

Dot and Marissa look at each other and then back to me. Dot says, "I told my mom I'd be home twenty minutes ago."

I say, "C'mon! She may already be gone," and then call out, "Bye, see you Monday!" to Phil and the nuns.

We run outside and I spot her backpack, bobbing back and forth about three blocks down Cook Street. "There she goes. C'mon!"

And I'm thinking we'll follow her to her house and then we'll know—she *does* have a home, she just doesn't have much money. But we follow her down Cook Street, all the way to College Street, across College, all the way to Bradley Road, and when she takes a left on Bradley, Dot says, "I can't go any farther. I've *got* to get home."

Marissa says, "Yeah, we could follow her clear out to Donovan at this rate. Why don't we just let her go?"

At this point I'm at least two miles from home and Grams is going to be getting pretty worried if I don't show up soon, but I've come this far and I figure the Girl's going to have to duck into a house pretty soon. So I say, "C'mon—just a few more blocks! She's got to live around here somewhere."

They look at each other, then give a quick nod. So off we go, ducking behind hedges and cars and whatever else we can find to hide behind, and pretty soon we're way out at Main Street, watching her walk under the freeway overpass.

Dot spots a pay phone. "Wait a sec! I'm going to call my mom."

While she's calling home, I keep an eye on that bobbing blue backpack, watching it get smaller and smaller. And just as I'm thinking we're going to lose her, Dot gets off the phone and says, "I've got to be home in forty minutes. Anyone else want to call? I've got change."

43

Marissa says, "Nah. No one but Mikey's going to be home anyway," because her parents are always gone, wheeling and dealing stocks at the office. And I want to say, "Nah," too, because I want to get *going,* but I grab the phone and say, "Follow her! I'll be right there."

Now, I don't lie to Grams. Sometimes I leave out important pieces of information, but I don't *lie.* So when she asks me, "Why are you going to be so late?" I say, "Marissa, Dot, and I are on our way over to a new friend's house. It won't take long. I just didn't want you to worry." Then before she can think of any questions to ask me I say, "I've got to go, Grams—they're waiting for me. See you soon. Bye!" and hang up the phone.

Dot and Marissa are already on the other side of the underpass so I run like crazy to catch up with them. "Where is she?"

They point across the street and Dot says, "See her? She's going through that field," and sure enough, there she is, stomping through the weeds.

Marissa says, "Where's she *going?* There aren't any houses out there, are there?"

I don't have a good answer for that. I've never gone stomping through fields at this end of town before. So I say, "Let's just follow her through the field and see where she goes. There's got to be something out there."

Marissa shakes her head. "There's nothing out there but the riverbed."

Dot says, "The riverbed? I didn't know Santa Martina had a river."

Marissa laughs. "It doesn't—it just has the bed."

Dot's looking at Marissa like she's got a few cracks in her carton of eggs, so Marissa says, "They built a dam a long time ago—up by Lake Chumash. Now there's only water in the river a few times a year, usually when the lake gets too full."

Dot says, "Ohhhh…"

We stand by a truck parked at the end of the street and wait, and when we're pretty sure we're going to lose her if we don't get moving, we start hurrying across the field.

The trouble with chasing someone across a field is, if they decide to turn around, you're caught. I mean, it's hard to hide or be inconspicuous when all you've got to work with is weeds.

And we weren't exactly being Indian scouts, either. Marissa kept swatting at gnats and picking prickers out of her socks. Dot kept snapping twigs, and I probably made the most noise of all, saying, "Shh! Shh!" at every little sound they made.

As we approached the riverbed, the plants got larger and bushier, which gave us something to duck behind. It also gave her something to disappear into.

At first I thought we'd lost her. All you could see in any direction were bushes. And when we stood stock-still, listening, all we could hear was the wind in the bushes. And that's when I realized that it was getting dark. In a hurry.

Then I noticed sort of a path where the weeds were mashed down. I whispered, "C'mon," and followed the trompled weeds.

We walked along like this for a few minutes, and then all of a sudden Dot grabs my shirt. I look at where she's pointing, and what I see down the riverbed is the Girl crawling into a box. A refrigerator box.

The box is on its side with tumbleweeds propped up around it, and except for a black Hefty bag peeking through the weeds on top, it looks pretty much like just another gnarly bush in a riverbed of tangled bushes.

We all stand there real close to each other, holding our breath. Marissa whispers, "She *lives* in there?"

I kind of nod. "Sure looks that way."

Dot says, "But she's *our* age!"

We stand there some more and finally I whisper, "So what do you want to do?"

Marissa whispers, "Sammy, no! I don't want to knock and say hello. You don't know anything about her. She might have a gun!"

Now, even though my first thought is to ask the Girl if she wants to come sneak by Mrs. Graybill and spend the night with me and Grams, I have to admit Marissa has a point. "Okay. So what do you want to do?"

Dot whispers, "It's getting dark. I think we should go back," and when Marissa nods and says, "So do I!" well, we tiptoe out of there as fast as we can.

And crossing back through the field you'd think we'd all be running off at the mouth about how this girl lives down by the riverbed in a refrigerator box, but we're not. We're as quiet as the stars, thinking. I'm sure Marissa was thinking about her room with the private bathroom and extra bed and all the glass furniture her mom makes her clean, and Dot was probably thinking about sharing a skinny little house with her parents and brothers and sisters, and how she's always wanted more privacy. I know I was thinking about having to live with Grams in the Senior Highrise and how I'm always complaining that it's not really a home, it's more like a refugee camp.

And walking back down Main Street in the dark with cars whizzing past, I shiver because it's cold out. It's very cold out. And it hits me that in all of Santa Martina there are probably only two girls who'd go to church in high-tops. Of those, one gets to sleep on her grandmother's couch.

The other has to spend the night in a cardboard box.

SIX

I didn't tell Grams about her. I just tried to act normal and went to bed early. But I know I had bad dreams, because when my cat, Dorito, jumped on the couch in the morning, I almost went through the roof, and it took me a minute to figure out just where I was.

And over breakfast Grams asked, "Are you all right?" because my oatmeal was setting up in front of me and I hadn't even touched my orange juice.

I was planning to say, "Sure," but what came out of my mouth was, "Grams, what would've happened to me if you hadn't taken me in?"

"What do you mean, dear? Of course I took you in. It's not like you're a stray cat or something. You're my granddaughter."

I sighed and asked, "Well, what if you hadn't been around? What do you think Mom would've done with me?"

Grams let out a nervous little laugh and said, "But I *am* around, Samantha. And I plan to be around for a long time, so you can put away those silly fears. You have nothing to worry about."

That didn't make me feel much better, but I didn't tell Grams that. I ate cold oatmeal and tried to act like everything was fine, and when it was time for me to sneak down to the Pup Parlor, I was glad to have something else to think about.

Marissa was already waiting, kind of rocking back and forth on her bike, and the first words out of her mouth were, "I couldn't sleep last night—could you? I can't believe she lives there."

I shook my head. "You didn't tell anyone, did you?"

"No."

"Good. Neither did I." And I'm about to ask her what she thinks we should do about it when I spot Dot.

Now, even though I'd never actually met Nibbles, in my mind I had a picture of what to expect. So when Dot comes flying down the sidewalk like a cat trying to water-ski, I almost can't believe that it's *her* dog towing her along. He's woollier than a mammoth and just about as big, and with all that hair hanging in his face he can't see where he's going because he's weaving back and forth when there is nothing to weave *around*.

Dot skids to a stop. "Sit, boy. *Sit!*"

Nibbles understands this to mean Wrap me up like a Maypole, because ten seconds later Dot's so tangled up she practically falls over.

Dot manages to choke out, "Hi!"

Marissa and I just stand there with our eyes bugged out and our chins down to our knees. "What *is* it?"

Dot laughs and says, "We think he's a cross between a sheepdog and a Great Dane. He was a really cute puppy, believe it or not. Mom says he's part kangaroo 'cause he jumps on everything, and part garbage disposal 'cause he eats everything."

Marissa shakes her head. "He looks like he could eat you out of house and home!"

"He does! He eats *everything*—and I don't mean just food. If you give him something on a paper plate, he'll eat the whole plate. He eats dolls and socks and pencils...anything."

By now Nibbles has figured out that he can get a good whiff of my baseball cap by kangarooing right there in front of me, so I back up and say, "What do you mean, 'eat'? He chews it up or he eats it?"

She yanks him back. "He *eats* it. Dad used to rush him off to the vet every time we'd catch him with half a toy in his mouth, but he's never really gotten sick or anything, so now when something's missing, we just figure it's in Nibbles' stomach and try to forget about it."

Marissa says, "I can't believe your mom even allows him in the *house*."

Dot shrugs. "He's not like this all the time. He's just excited to be out. At home he's not much worse than my brothers." She yanks on the leash and says, "I'm going to take him inside now—want to come?"

I say, "Sure!" because I like the Pup Parlor. Sometimes I go there on my way home from school just to see what kind of foo-foo dogs Vera and Meg are busy wrestling with. I'm talking the kind that won't eat unless you're serving filet mignon in a crystal dish. It's fun seeing one of *them* go down for a flea dip. Their condescending little eyes pop wide open and they start panicking like mice in a snake pit. And when it's all over and they're dry and caged up with little red bows in their hair, they're not thinking about how nice they look or how good they smell. No, they're busy plotting out what piece of furniture they're going to wet on when they get home.

I also like going to the Pup Parlor because Vera and Meg like to have me. They always say, "Good afternoon, Sammy!" and after they get done cooing about some new stray they've taken in, asking me things like, "You know anyone who wants to take in this darlin' little fellow?" or "You sure your grandma doesn't have room for this one? He don't eat much—he just needs some lovin'," they make me tell them all about the big bad world of William Rose Junior High School. They actually *like* to hear about it.

And I guess maybe I talk a little too much to them because they figured out about me living at the Highrise. I didn't actually *tell* them, they just pieced it together. Grams had a fit when I told her they knew—said something about the circle getting too large. But I swore them to secrecy, and I think they'd sooner put themselves out of house and home than do that to me.

Vera's the one I like the best. She's Meg's mom and she's about sixty years old and as wiry as a whippet. I've never known a lady as strong as Vera. She can get a samoyed in the tub single-handed and can strip an entire husky faster than most people can fix their own hair. She wears an apron, but she's always covered with dog hair anyway, and you can tell by looking at her hands that she'd as soon use dog clippers on her nails as let them get in her way.

She *does* spend time on her own hair, though. She and Meg both wear a little red bow on each side of their heads and I always kind of wonder whether they go to a beauty parlor with a picture of a poodle and say, "I want to look like this," or if they just get down and do each other's hair right there in the shop.

Meg's a lot like Vera in that she can dip a mastiff quicker than you or I could corner a schnauzer, but she doesn't really look much like Vera. Even with her hair colored the same as Vera's and even with those little bows decorating it, Meg looks like a bulldog pretending to be a poodle.

Anyway, when Nibbles goes charging inside and knocks the HELP WANTED sign out of the window, Vera just puts it back up and says, "Good morning, girls!" She pushes the hair away from Nibbles' eyes, saying, "Hello there, fella. So you've got some nasty critters chewing you up—we'll take care of that."

Meg takes the leash from Dot and says, "Try back at one o'clock. We should have him combed out by then."

So Marissa locks up her bike and off we go, walking down Broadway and along Cook Street to the library, around the lawn bowlers and past the kiddie swings to the back end of the ball park. And while we're walking, we're talking about Nibbles and the Pup Parlor and how nice Meg and Vera are.

But the minute we get down to the diamond and start throwing the ball around, Dot says, "I had a dream about her last night," and right away we know—she's talking about the Girl.

I say, "Oh, yeah?"

Dot throws me the ball. "Yeah. She was on one side of

this glass door and I was on the other. And she was acting like she wanted to come through, but she didn't have a doorknob, and every time I tried mine, the knob kept slipping." The ball snaps into her glove and she says, "It was really frustrating."

Marissa runs her arm in a circle like a windmill. "I wonder where her parents are."

Dot says, "Maybe she's like a juvenile delinquent or something. My mom says some kids are just bad."

Marissa and I freeze and say at the same time, "You didn't tell her, did you?"

Dot says, "No, no! I didn't tell her....I just asked her, you know, how come some of the people at the soup kitchen are so young."

Marissa and I groan, but Dot says, "She didn't have any idea I was talking about some*body*. I didn't say a word about following her to the riverbed or anything. Honest!" She lets out a nervous laugh. "She would've killed me!"

We get back to throwing the ball around and finally I say, "So what are we going to do about it?"

Marissa knows I'm thinking about the extra bed in her room because she throws me the ball and says, "Sammy, what if she *is* a juvenile delinquent? I can't just invite her to come stay with me! She might rob us blind, and then what am I supposed to do? Say, Oh, sorry, Mom, I was just trying to be nice...?"

Dot says, "I'd talk to my mom about it, but where would she go? We don't have enough room as it is, and Mom would probably wind up calling Social Services or something."

I sigh, "Well *I* can't take her in. I'd wind up out there *with* her if Mrs. Graybill caught on."

So we just stand there in a triangle, throwing the ball around and finally Marissa says, "Look, we can't do anything about it right now. What we *can* do something about is Monday's game. Everybody's expecting us to choke, and I want to get out there and prove them wrong." She looks right at me. "Sammy, we've got to work on our signals, and I've got a couple more I want to show you. Dot, we've got to work on drilling them home from third. You tend to throw them a little outside, and that can make it hard for Sammy to make the tag."

When Marissa McKenze gets down to business, *you* get down to business, too. She's not bossy, she's just serious. And you don't mind her telling you you need work on your signals or throwing from the hole—she knows what she's doing and you listen. At least I do, and so does Dot. The eighth graders seem to think she's got a little too much salt on her popcorn, but that's their loss.

So we got down to work, and for a couple of hours I forgot about the Girl and concentrated on beating Heather's team. And when Marissa finally breaks into a grin and says, "Okay! Now we're clicking! What do you say we go to Juicers and get a couple of dogs—my treat," Dot and I say, "Yahoo!" and off we go to the mall.

And I'm laughing about how we're going to rake Heather's team through the chalk, when I see Marissa's cousin Brandon. I don't know what it is about Brandon, but whenever I'm around him my words get all twisted up and I spend a lot of time looking at my high-tops and acting like I'm about six years old. And it's not like I have a crush on him or anything. I mean, he's cute and all, but he's a hotshot on the high school swim team, and the last thing in the world I'd have is a crush on a hotshot.

It's probably just because he's so nice to me that my tongue gets all mixed up. I mean I *am* Marissa's best friend and he *is* her cousin, so he just acts like I'm one of the family, which is nice, but my tongue would be a lot happier if he'd just ignore me.

We get up to the counter and he says, "Hey, cuz. Hi, Dot," and then, "Hiya, Sammy!" to me. And he's about to ask me, "How's life?" like he always does so I can sputter like an idiot, but then he notices my mitt. He reaches over and takes it from me. "Cool!" He pounds his fist in it a couple of times and says, "It's kind of big for you, isn't it?"

I just shrug and say, "No."

See what I mean? What kind of a stupid answer is No?

He hands me back the mitt and says to Marissa, "Mom says you guys made it to the playoffs. You're the under-dogs?"

Marissa starts talking a mile a minute. "Yeah, but we're gonna show them. We've got strategy, we've got speed, Sammy and I are clickin'. We're gonna close them out on Monday—you just wait and see."

Brandon grins and says, "Well, I'll be rooting for you." Then he looks us all over. "Is this a social visit or can I get you something to eat?"

Marissa orders us hot dogs and drinks, and when we've

polished off every last bite and slurped up every drop, we wave bye to Brandon and head back to the Pup Parlor.

What I notice first when I walk in the door are the bows in Meg's hair. They're all cockeyed, and one of them's dangling from a single hair. She sees us and calls, "They're here, Mom!"

Vera pops up from behind the counter, shaking her head, and even though her bows are nice and tidy, she's looking very, very tired. She says to Meg, "I've tried every key on this chain. None of 'em work."

I can see Nibbles panting away in a drying cage, and it doesn't *look* like they've had any trouble dipping the woolly beast, but from the angle of Meg's bows and the look on Vera's face I know something's gone wrong. "What happened?"

Meg shakes her head. "That dog ate the key to our safe."

Dot's hand flies up to her mouth. "He ate *what?*"

Vera says, "The key to our safe. We don't have an extra one and I don't know how in the world we're going to get the thing open. We've got a week's worth of deposits in there!"

"How did he get the key to your *safe?*"

Meg says, "He broke away from Mom, and the next thing you know he's got the place turned upside down and he's eating the key."

Vera holds up a plastic dog-bone key chain like it's a prize-winning trout. The key end is missing, and the dog bone is looking pretty mangled. "I pried this out of him, but the rest is gone."

Well, I know it's not funny, but I can just see Vera with

her hand halfway down Nibbles' throat, diving in for that key, and I'm having the hardest time not laughing. Then Meg says to Dot, "You're just going to have to look for it."

Dot stares at her. "*Look* for it? What do you mean?"

Meg shrugs and says, "It'll come through—probably late today or tomorrow—and when it does, just clean it up and bring it back."

Now, Dot's thinking, There's no *way,* but what comes out of her mouth is, "Have you called a locksmith?"

"Yeah, and they want an arm and a leg to open and key it." She shakes her head. "It's no big deal. Just check for it when you clean up after him, and scrub up good when you're done."

Dot looks at me like, *Help,* so I say, "What about the combination? Isn't that written down anywhere?"

Meg pulls the dangling bow out of her hair. "That died with Dad. All we've ever had's the key." She pops the bow back in her hair and says, "Look, you can pay for the locksmith if you want. All we're asking is that you check for the key."

We all kind of look at each other, not saying anything. Finally, Dot's eyes crinkle closed and she says, "Okay… okay. I'll look for it."

Dot pays them for dipping Nibbles, and when Vera clips his leash on and hands him over she says, "He's a nice one, even if he is a bit of a maniac."

As soon as we get outside, Marissa whispers, "Are you really going to do it?"

Nibbles starts walking Dot down the street and she calls over her shoulder, "What choice do I have? Maybe Dad'll pay for the locksmith, but I doubt it." She yanks on the leash and mutters, "Stupid dog!"

So Dot goes to report the big news to her parents, and Marissa heads back to the mall to play video games. And I was planning just to go home and check in with Grams, but about halfway up the fire escape stairs I got the bright idea that I might know someone who could save Dot from having to dissect dog poop.

At least, I thought, it was worth a shot.

SEVEN

Hudson Graham likes to talk about himself. He does it all the time. But what I've been noticing lately is that even though I know a lot about his seventy-two years, there's also a lot I *don't* know. And it seems there are some things I'll ask him but never really get an answer for. Like, What are you doing with so many tape recorders? and Why do you have dictionaries in so many languages? He'll start telling me some interesting story, but lots of times it winds up not having anything to do with my question. The better I get to know Hudson, the more I think that maybe he worked for the CIA. Either that or he was a politician, I haven't quite decided. Either way, I figured that if anyone knew how to crack a safe, it'd be Hudson Graham.

He was sitting on his porch with his boots kicked up on the rail, reading a magazine, and his dachshund Rommel was curled up next to his chair. Rommel flipped his tail a few times when he saw me coming, which made Hudson look up from his reading. "Sammy! What a nice surprise."

I ruffled Rommel's ears and ducked down to see the name of Hudson's magazine. "*Large Format*...what's that about?"

Hudson sits up, then flips the magazine closed and shows me the cover. "It's about view cameras and large-format photography." He can tell I don't know what he's talking about so he says, "Instead of a negative the size of a cracker, large-format photographers deal with negatives the size of this magazine."

"Is that why you've got a darkroom?"

He grins and says, "I've been known to dabble," and then changes the subject. "So, I was thinking about asking Rita to church with me tomorrow. Do you think she'd be interested?"

Now, my grandmother likes to go to church, all right, and she doesn't like to go alone, which is how I usually get dragged into it. And since I'd been spending so much time at St. Mary's after school, I sure didn't want to go there on Sunday. So I say, "Sounds like a great idea to me!"

Hudson kicks his reptile-looking boots back on the rail. "What do you think? The ten o'clock mass?"

I plop my high-tops right next to his boots and say, "Good choice. Ten's when she likes to go."

He points to my shoes. "You got new ones!"

I laugh and say, "Yup," and then point to his boots. "So did you! Let me guess—alligator?"

He laughs, "Guess again."

"I don't know...snake? Boa constrictor?"

"You're stabbing at it, child. Take it slow—color, texture, pattern. Try again."

I reach over and touch them and they don't feel soft like snake. They feel rougher, more sturdy. "Okay, it's some kind of reptile."

"Go on."

"Too tough for snake and too soft for alligator or crocodile."

"Go on."

"It's something in between—like maybe a lizard."

He just sits there smiling at me.

I study them some more. "Is that the natural color? I've never seen a green lizard."

"Keep your mind open, Sammy. Keep it open."

Suddenly, it clicks. "It's iguana!"

He gives me a great big smile, "Panamanian iguana—good girl!" He gets up and says, "I'm going to give your grandmother a call. Should I tell her you're here?"

Well, I think that's a real good idea because it'll keep me from having to explain to her *why* I'm there. And since Hudson doesn't know yet, he can't tell her. I say, "Sure. And tell her I won't be home for a couple of hours, okay?"

He raises one of his bushy white eyebrows at me, but then just ducks inside. When he comes back a few minutes later, he says, "We're all set." He kicks his lizard feet back up on the railing and grins. "And guess who's chaperoning?"

It takes me a second, but finally I get it. "Oh *no!* Why?"

Hudson's still grinning. "She insists."

I roll my eyes and mutter, "Like I haven't spent enough time there this week."

He gives me an Oh? kind of look, so I tell him about how I'm working off my detention scrubbing the church down and helping out in the soup kitchen, and that the last thing I want to do is spend my day off listening to Father Mayhew talk about finding the high road to Heaven.

Hudson runs his hand along Rommel's back. "Hmm. That's got to be a fairly enlightening experience—working on the inside of the temple of God."

I laugh. "You sound just like Sister Bernice!"

He looks at me. "Sister Bernice? I only know Josephine and Mary Margaret."

So I tell him all about Bernice and the Sisters of Mercy, and how they're doing a fundraiser for St. Mary's. When I'm all done, he laughs and says, "This I have got to see. Do you think they'll be at church tomorrow?"

"I don't know. All I know is they're supposed to give these big performances at the end of the week, and Monday I've got to help them stuff envelopes."

Hudson studies me and says, "So what's on your mind, Sammy?" He taps my baseball cap. "I can feel a question cooking up there. What is it?"

I take a deep breath. "Don't think I'm being nosy here, okay?" He gives me a little nod so I say, "I was just wondering whether you knew anything about safecracking."

He raises an eyebrow, then smoothes it with a finger as it comes back down. "Why do you ask?"

So I tell him. All about Dot and Nibbles and the key to Meg and Vera's safe, and how Dot's going to have to spend the next couple of days dissecting dog poop.

He eyes me and says, "So you're thinking maybe I can take a stethoscope to the safe, twist the knob a few times, and *poof,* it'll open right up?"

I kind of shrug. "I don't know. I thought maybe you had some, uh, you know…experience?"

He throws back his head and laughs, and I'm expecting

him to shake his head and say, Sammy, Sammy, Sammy…
like he does when I'm being dopey, but when he stops
laughing, he says, "It just so happens I *do* know a little
about safecracking, but—"

"You *do?* Can you go over there and crack theirs open?"

Hudson laughs, "Whoa, whoa! Slow down there a
minute, Sammy. There are some things you need to understand about your options before you decide on the
best course of action."

I wait while he dusts some imaginary dirt off the tip of
his boot. Then he looks at me and says, "On your typical
S&G lock you've got a dial with hash marks that run from
zero to ninety-nine. If you took every configuration of
those numbers for a three-number combination, you're
looking at a million possible combinations. Literally. So
setting out to try every one would take ages. But on most
dials there's a considerable margin of error. For example,
if one of the numbers is two, then three and four will
probably work if you overshoot in one direction, and zero
and one will probably work if you overshoot in the other.
Depends on how sloppy the mechanism is. So really you
only need to try one out of five numbers—like 0, 5, 10,
15, 20, and so on. Let's say the combination is 3–23–56.
Or 4–23–56 or 5–23–56 or 6–23–56. 5–25–55 will probably work for all of them or any other combination within
the mechanism's margin of error. You get the idea. So
now the right combination isn't one in a million, it's
about one in seven or eight thousand. Something you
could do in a day or two."

Now when I thought of Hudson helping me open the

safe, I wasn't picturing having to flip around a dial for hours and hours. I was picturing Hudson going into the Pup Parlor with a few tools and some experienced fingers, and coming out with the doggy door wide open.

He looks at me and says, "Not exactly what you were hoping to hear, eh, Sammy?" He chuckles and says, "It may seem rather dull to you, but a yegg's best tool's his brain." He taps my head and says, "It's better than a crowbar or a diamond drill or a truckload of nitroglycerin, so don't you roll your eyes and sigh at me, young lady! It's probably the only thing that's going to get you past an S&G lock, nearly an inch of reinforced steel and shielded bolts."

I sit up. "I didn't roll my eyes and sigh!" Then I kind of mumble, "But it's not like I want to break into Fort Knox!"

He shakes his head. "Sammy, Sammy, Sammy...Some safes may be easier than others, but the concept's the same. Stethoscopes and cracker fingers are a myth. You can't get into a safe that way! And torching the mechanism or trying to drill it is just going to make it lock up.

"Which leaves you with ripping a hole in the side or using your brain." He eyes me. "Which do you prefer?"

I guess I wasn't looking too happy because he says, "Come on now, Sammy. Chin up."

"I don't want to try eight thousand different combinations! I'd rather dissect dog poop!"

He laughs. "Well, there *is* another way to go at this."

"What do you mean?"

"It comes down to the fact that people are creatures of habit."

"How's that get you into a safe?"

"Imagine, if you will, that for your birthday I gave you a brand-new Browning safe and you had to decide on a combination that you wanted the lock to have. It could be any combination of three numbers, zero to ninety-nine. What would you choose?"

"Doesn't the safe come with a combination?"

Hudson laughs, and says, "Ah-ha! Very good! Choice number one—the factory setting. Usually along the lines of 25–0–25, and the first combination you should try when confronted with a lock."

"What do you mean?"

He smiles. "People are also lazy. Some will leave the combination on the factory setting because it's too much work for them to figure out how to give the safe a new combination." He rubs his hands together. "But you are *not* lazy, so you would come up with your own combination. What would it be?"

I'm in the middle of thinking when he says, "Would you pick random numbers? Say, 17–85–12?"

"No. I'd forget them—unless I wrote them down."

He claps his hands. "Another possibility! If it's a random combination, or one that they're afraid they're going to forget, most people write it down and then put it someplace concealed but convenient. Like they write it inside their desk drawer or tape it to the back of their safe." He laughs and says, "There's not much sense in having a safe if you're going to tape the combination to the outside of it, but people do it all the time."

He goes back to petting Rommel. "Now, I know you've

got more marbles than to do that, so what combination *would* you use? And remember—this safe is something you're going to have for a long, long time."

I sit there for a minute, thinking. Then I say, "12–34–56. That's what I'd use. 12–34–56."

Hudson stops mid-stroke. "Twelve–thirty-*four*–fifty-six?"

"That's right."

"It's not a date, then."

"Nope."

He picks Rommel up and puts him in his lap. "Okay. I give up. Why that combination?"

I laugh. "I couldn't think of anything. You were putting me on the spot, so I just went up the number line!"

He gives me a disgusted look. "I suppose I should've known you wouldn't be conventional. Most people don't go up the number line, Sammy. *Most* people choose a memorable date of some kind, like their birthday or their spouse's birthday or their anniversary. That's the most common thing people use. Then comes the first digits of their Social Security number or their phone number—something along those lines. A number that has to do with some other aspect of their life."

He lets a little smile escape. "The more you know about someone, the easier it is to crack their safe, so what I suggest you do with Meg and Vera is find out everything you can about them, write it all down, and then look for combinations. Find combinations in everything they give you. And Sammy, keep your mind open. If you keep your mind open, I predict you'll have it cracked in under an hour."

He laughs and says, "And if you *can't* get it open, then I guess Dot'll have to do her dirty deed, which isn't the end of the world."

So I walk away from Hudson's without so much as a water glass to put up to the dial, and the closer I get to the Pup Parlor, the more I'm thinking that maybe Hudson's never cracked a safe in his life. I mean, what he'd told me about safecracking sounded like something you'd get out of a statistics book, not the Safecracker's Bible.

When I walk into the Pup Parlor and Meg says, "Sammy! What brings you back so soon?" I really felt like saying, Uh...never mind, but what came out of my stupid mouth was, "I'm here to crack your safe."

They both stare at me. And then Meg starts laughing. And pretty soon she's laughing so hard that her little red bows are shaking around her poodle-do like mutant moths and she just has to sit down. Finally, she wipes the corners of her eyes and says, "I'm sorry, Sammy. It's been a long day."

Vera comes from behind the counter. "What makes you think you can open the safe?"

I look down and say, "I don't know. I just have an idea about it, all right? Will you at least let me try?"

Vera looks at Meg and they both kind of shrug. "Have at it, girl."

I pick up a pencil and a scratch pad and say to Vera, "You have to give me some information."

"Like?"

"Like your husband's birth date, your birth date, Meg's birth date, your anniversary, your phone number, everyone's Social Security number, your driver's license number, your husband's driver's license number..."

Meg shakes her head. "My father's driver's license number? Why do you need that?"

But Vera nods and says, "This makes sense. I should've tried this years ago. I just always had the key." And before you know it, she's giving me dates and numbers and I've got a whole paper full of combinations to try.

I sit cross-legged on the floor and I start, first with his birthday, then with Vera's. And it feels kind of funny, sitting in front of someone else's safe twirling the dial around while they're standing behind you shaking their heads, muttering. And the more combinations I try, the louder Meg mutters until finally I'm out of combinations and she comes right out and says, "I knew it wouldn't work."

Well, I am feeling pretty stupid, but I'm not quite ready to give up. I sit there thinking, and then I ask, "Have you always lived at this address?"

Vera says, "Yup."

"Has your phone number always been the same?"

"Yup...wait, no! We had one way back when—let me see...2-2812. Yup that was it. Walnut 2-2812."

"Walnut? What do you mean 'Walnut'?"

Meg says, "When I was your age, that's how we used to say phone numbers. The WA in Walnut translates to 92. Look at the phone—that's what the letters are there for."

I pick up the phone and sure enough, ABC is on 2 and WXY is on 9.

Vera says, "Yeah, that was back when you just needed the last five numbers."

"What do you mean? You didn't have to dial the nine and the two?"

She shakes her head. "Our number was 22812. You could dial the WA if you wanted to, but no one did it. No need for it."

This was all news to me, but I wasn't going to stand around and chat about how things used to be. I went right back over to the safe and tried 22–81–2, and as I turned the dial around to 2, I pulled down on the handle and...nothing. I said, "Darn!" Then I tried 22–8–12, and shook the handle when it didn't give.

There was only one combination left. I spun the dial around a couple of times, then very carefully went clockwise to the number 2, back to 28, and as I got back to 12, I pulled the handle down.

And there I was, with the door to their safe swung open in my lap.

EIGHT

Meg was surprised more than happy about the lock, probably because of all that muttering she'd done about me not being able to open it. And seeing how it was gaping at her like a baby bird needing bugs, she couldn't really *say* much.

But Vera says, "That's amazing! I can't believe it actually worked! Why, all this time it was our old phone number."

Meg picks up a broom and starts sweeping. "Yeah, and now we're gonna have to get the combination changed."

I look at her and say, "I won't tell anyone what it is!"

Vera says, "This is *Sammy*, Meg. She's more trustworthy than a locksmith, and I don't think I need to remind you that she's trusted us with a few secrets of her own."

Meg keeps sweeping up dog hair and pretty soon she sighs and says, "You're right. I'm sorry." She looks at me. "Ma and I are much obliged, Sammy."

Vera says, "And if there's ever anything we can do for you, just let us know."

I head home, and after I sneak past Mrs. Graybill the first thing I do is call Hudson and say, "Thanks!" And I can just see him, smiling like a silver fox, when he says, "That's my girl!"

I call Dot and say, "Guess what? You are officially off poop patrol!" and let me tell you, that is one happy girl.

All night I had so many dreams about spinning dials

'round and around that when Grams woke me up in the morning, it took my brain a second to quit feeling dizzy.

After we're done cleaning up from breakfast and it's time to get going, Grams says what she always does when she drags me to church, "We have *got* to get you some decent shoes."

And I say what I always say, "If I can't wear my high-tops, I'm not going."

She just sighs, and we head over to Hudson's.

When we get there, he answers the door and says, "Good morning, ladies," then winks at me and says, "Perfect day for church, isn't it?"

I laugh and say, "Perfect," because it is—it's overcast and gloomy. Then I point to his boots and say, "Even your feet are ready to be bored," because they're not wearing yellow pigskin or green iguana. They're stuck in black cowhide.

He smiles at Grams and says, "Do we have time for a cup of tea? I've got the water hot."

Grams stays put on the porch. "I'd like to get a good seat. Maybe afterwards?"

As we pass the statue of the Virgin Mary on the church walkway, out of the corner of my eye I notice Father Mayhew by a side door. And I do a double take, because he's talking to a police officer—Officer Gil Borsch.

Now, my feet were smart—they tried to keep on walking. It's kind of a long story, but to Officer Borsch I'm like a swig of sour milk that he can't spit out. If he had his way, he'd spray me all over the walls, but the way things are he just has to swallow and wait for the upset stomach to go away.

So I probably should've kept on walking, only I could tell that Father Mayhew was really upset about something. So I say, "Save me a seat, Grams. I'll be right there."

Father Mayhew seems happy enough to see me, but Officer Borsch takes one look at me and mutters, "Tell me this isn't happening."

I decide I'm going to be nice to the guy, just to see what happens. "Good morning, Officer Borsch. How is everything?"

He looks at me like I'm going to pull a squirt gun from behind my back, but since I just stand there smiling, he finally grunts and says, "Things have been worse."

I look at Father Mayhew and ask, "What's happened? Is something else missing?"

Officer Borsch squints a bit. "Something *else*?"

Father Mayhew closes his eyes and sighs. "My papal cross disappeared earlier this week. It was in the sacristy also. Perhaps the person who took the chalices also has my cross." He shakes his head. "I should probably also mention that our guests, the Sisters of Mercy, have had an attempted break-in in their motor home."

While Officer Borsch is writing all this down, I whisper, "What else got taken?"

Father Mayhew says, "Two Eucharistic goblets. I just can't believe it. All these years and we've never had an iota of trouble. Now in less than a week we've had three incidents."

Officer Borsch looks up from his writing. "You mentioned they were gold—gold plate or solid?"

Father Mayhew looks down. "Solid."

Officer Borsch lets out a low whistle. "And you never lock that room up?"

"Only at night. We've kept them there for years. Years and years. As a matter of fact, they were here when I was assigned to the parish nearly twenty years ago." His eyebrows practically knit together and his complicated eyes look sad and confused. "Please do your best to find out who has stolen these things. It's more than their monetary or even their sentimental value. Not knowing casts a shadow on the church. A long, dark shadow." He looks at his watch and says, "It's time for me to go. Maybe I could speak with you more after Mass? I'll come to the station if you'd like."

Officer Borsch agrees, and while Father Mayhew ducks through the side door, I head back to the front door, calling over my shoulder, "Good luck, Officer Borsch!"

He doesn't quite know what to say to that, so he just grunts and goes back to writing in his notebook.

When I spot Grams at the front of the church, I go up and take my seat like a good little girl, and just as Grams is about to ask me where I'd gone, someone attacks the organ and we all practically jump through the roof.

Now you have to understand, they don't usually have an organist at St. Mary's. Someone'll strum a guitar while everyone sings "Chorus of Faith" or "Amazing Grace," but that's about as noisy as we get.

So having a seat near the organ pipes has never been dangerous before, but there I was, peeling myself off the ceiling. Then I notice that behind the organ is Sister Clarice, pounding away and rocking out like Barbie Bebop.

Then all of a sudden Bernice's voice is booming, "When Heaven, when Heaven calls your name..." from one side of the church, and Abigail's voice is echoing, "When Heaven, when Heaven calls your name..." from the other. And I'm smiling, because this is more awake than I've *ever* been in church.

Then Sister Bernice and Sister Abigail come swaying through the congregation and over to the organ with their hands up in the air, singing, "I said, Heaven, when Heaven calls your name...You gonna be ready? When Heaven calls your name. Let me hear you now, Heaven! When Heaven calls your name!"

Some people are starting to clap along with the music, but most people are just whispering to each other like they can't quite believe what's happening in their church.

I hear Grams say to Hudson, "Good heavens! What *is* this?"

Hudson says back, "Something this church has needed for a long time!" He starts clapping along, singing, "Heaven, when Heaven calls your name...You gonna be ready?" and while he's singing and clapping, he nudges Grams and looks at her like, C'mon, Rita! Loosen up and have some fun!

Well, before you know it, there's my grandmother, clapping her hands in church, kind of looking around to make sure that no one she knows is watching. And pretty soon I hear her voice singing, "Heaven, when Heaven calls your name...You gonna be ready? When Heaven calls your name."

By the time Father Mayhew walks up to the pulpit, the

bricks of the church are practically shaking in their mortar from all that singing and clapping. Of course, there are still some old people looking around like they just bit into a green persimmon, but when Father Mayhew says, "May the Lord be with you," everyone practically shouts, "And also with you!" like they're happy and they really mean it.

After the opening prayer, Father Mayhew says, "This time of year brings, for many of us, great joy. It is a time for giving thanks, and most of us have much to be thankful for. For family, for friends, for our good health and the comfort of our homes. Even for the lessons, however hard they may have been, that we have learned on our journey through the past year. As for myself, I am thankful for all of you. For your faith, for your dedication to your church. For your charity and willingness to believe in a higher cause.

"Our work, though, is never done. Each year it seems we see more hunger, more need for human kindness, and, yes, more despair. The Church does its best to address those needs, but often our efforts fall short."

Father Mayhew is quiet for a minute. Then he says, "Last month after a long talk with God about what more I could do to help the unfortunate through the coming winter, I received a letter from a touring group of Sisters, asking if our parish would be interested in having them do a series of concerts as a fundraiser. Attached to the letter was a stack of recommendations and copies of newspaper reviews, and after reading how successful these Sisters have been in raising money for the needy, I realized that my prayers had been answered."

He looks over at the organ and smiles. "Our guests for the week are Sisters Bernice, Abigail, and Clarice. They're known as the Sisters of Mercy and it is their mission to raise enough funds to see every needy person in Santa Martina through the winter."

The Sisters of Mercy smile at us from over by the organ, and then Father Mayhew says, "It is my hope that you will support them in any way you can. Talk to people you know in the community, let them know why the Sisters are here, and encourage them to attend the shows. They will be giving performances on Thursday, Friday, and Saturday of this week, and although you'll read about them in the paper and see them interviewed on television, the very best way for us to have a successful drive is word of mouth. We need your help and I know I can count on each and every one of you to provide it."

Now, I hadn't noticed it before, but Sister Josephine and Sister Mary Margaret are in the row in front of us, down toward the aisle. Sister Mary Margaret's sitting very still with her hands in her lap, but Sister Josephine is gripping her cane like she's going to get up and leave any minute. And when the organ blasts again and the Sisters of Mercy start up on a new song, well, Mary Margaret and Josephine can't seem to stop whispering back and forth to each other, buzzing like flies in a barnyard.

And I was so busy thinking about Mary Margaret and Josephine, and how funny it was that nuns could treat other nuns the way eighth graders treat seventh graders, that I didn't really tune back in until Father Mayhew was going through the Eucharistic Prayer and I heard the goblet he was using clink against the dish with the wafers on it.

It was the clink that made me quit thinking about Nun Wars and look up at the communion table. It was the clink that made me forget all about singing in church and remember the missing goblets.

And when I remembered where I'd heard that sound before, my heart started bouncing around in my chest and my hands started going clammy. And the more I thought about it, the more sure I was that I knew who had taken Father Mayhew's goblets.

And who had taken his cross.

NINE

It wasn't hard getting away from Grams and Hudson. They were so wrapped up in the Sisters of Mercy that they didn't even ask me where I was going when I said, "See you back home in a while."

I took Church Street to Bradley, across to Main, and then under the freeway. And about halfway across the field I started thinking that calling Dot or Marissa would have been a better idea than taking off on my own. I mean, it was the middle of the day and there were cars and people buzzing all along Main Street, but I couldn't really hear them anymore. And the farther away from the street I got, the quieter it was and the more I was wishing Marissa and Dot were with me so at least I could tell them "Shh! Shh!" and *hear* something.

By the time I got to the bushes, my heart was flopping around like a goldfish in grass. I snuck from one bush to the next, looking for any sign of the Girl, and when I got close enough to see the box, I crawled behind a bush and waited. And waited and waited some more. And when I was sure she didn't know I was there, I started tossing rocks.

The first couple landed in the sand in front of the box,

and the next one didn't really connect because it was blocked by a tumbleweed. But then I landed one, *whack*, against the front flap.

I waited another minute, and when she didn't come out, I decided it was time for me to go in. I scrambled down the bank and when I got to the box, I stood to one side and pulled open the flap. Now, I'm half expecting to see the Girl sitting there, ready to blow my brains out, but what I see instead is an old down sleeping bag, a pile of clothes, and a paper sack.

The paper sack is full, but I can't tell of what. And I'm thinking that maybe the goblets and cross are stashed inside it, so I take a quick look over both shoulders and dive inside.

When the flap comes down, it's suddenly *dark* inside. And it smells wet. Wet and musty—like old magazines in a basement. And I don't know if it was the Hefty bag on the roof keeping all the moisture in or if all refrigerator boxes smell that bad after a while, but the place was in serious need of some ventilation.

After a minute my eyes got used to the darkness, so I crawled over to the grocery sack and opened it up. And what's inside? Cans. No cross, no goblets, just cans of food. Pineapple, macaroni and cheese, beans, stew, and spaghetti. Lots of spaghetti. And next to the cans is an old can opener and a spoon.

I give up on the bag and try the pile of clothes, but there's nothing in that, either. Just an old pair of jeans, a couple of shirts and a jacket. And I'm just about to put the clothes back the way I'd found them when I notice writing on the inside of the jacket. I flip it back open and there on the label is HOLLY JANQUELL.

So. Her name was Holly. I flipped the jacket over and realized that maybe I was jumping to conclusions. Maybe this was just a jacket she'd gotten from the Salvation Army.

I probably should've just backed right out of there—I mean, I didn't see the cross or the goblets, and that *was* why I was there. But I couldn't quit wondering whether Holly Janquell was a girl who owned nothing but one jacket, one sleeping bag, and a sack of canned spaghetti, or if she was a girl with so many jackets that she could give one away to the Salvation Army and never miss it. So I started looking for something else with a name on it.

And there I am, pawing through the clothes, when light comes flooding into the box. I turn around and find myself looking straight up the blade of a knife

I'm not talking pocketknife. I'm talking you could gut a grizzly with this thing. It's grafted with duct tape to one end of a broomstick, and practically grafted to the other end is the Girl.

She doesn't say a word. She just looks at me like I'm a big ugly roach in her house, and she's Raid. I yank the sleeping bag in front of me for some kind of feeble protection, and yell, "Wait! Wait, you don't understand!" And as I'm looking for that spear to come gashing through feathers, I take a gamble and say, "Holly! Holly, put it down. I'm sorry! I'm *sorry.*"

Nothing happens, so I sneak a peek around the side of the bag. She's glaring at me and that skewer of hers isn't even quivering. It just keeps pointing right at my chest while she shuffles into a better position.

Before she can shish-kebab me, I blurt out, "Holly, please. Just put it down. I'm not here to hurt you or steal anything, I..."

She jabs her spear forward a few inches. "Who sent you here?"

I shrink back a little. "Nobody. Honest!"

She comes in another couple of inches. "Those nosy nuns sent you, didn't they?"

I'm trying to figure out the best way to bust a back door in this box when she says, "How'd they find out my name?"

I drop the sleeping bag and pick up her jacket. "It's written right here! Nobody sent me, I'm just here 'cause I thought you might have Father Mayhew's goblets and cross. He thought *I* took his cross and it's real important to him that he gets it back. I'm sorry, okay? I was wrong."

She keeps right on crouching in front of me, but I can see a little doubt tiptoeing around her eyes.

I whisper, "I'm sorry, okay?" I put the jacket down and put my hands up. "I didn't mean any harm. Really."

She studies me some more and then says, "This... is...my *home*."

I look down. "I know. I just thought..."

She moves the knife a little closer to me. "You thought breaking into a box wouldn't be the same thing as breaking into somebody's house, didn't you? You thought tearing through my stuff wouldn't be like going through someone's dresser, didn't you? You probably live in some cushy little house and sleep on a cushy little bed and have dinner put in front of your face every night—"

"No! I don't! I live with my grandmother in an apartment where kids aren't even allowed! I've got to sneak up and down the fire escape stairs so no one will know I'm there. I sleep on the couch and all the stuff I own fits in one tiny drawer in my grandmother's dresser." I look around and say real quietly, "Maybe I don't live in a box, and maybe I don't eat cold spaghetti for dinner, but there's no way I have it *cushy*." I give her half a smile. "I wouldn't switch with you, but I'd trade your cold spaghetti for Grams' lima bean casserole any day!"

She glares at me, kind of biting the side of her cheek. Then she asks, "So why you living there?"

"My mom decided she had better things to do than take care of me." The knife's starting to come down a little, so I take a deep breath and say, "How'd you wind up here?"

Her spear pops right back up. "It's none of your business! And you may think you're like me, but you're not. You're just like the rest of them: Something's missing? I saw that homeless girl hangin' around. Must be her."

"No...I..."

She jabs the knife forward. "Shut up!"

While she's busy thinking of what she's going to do with me, I try to scramble up a reason for her not to kill me. "We followed you out here yesterday."

She squints at me. *"We?"*

"Yeah. Me and my friends, Marissa and Dot."

She blinks at me a few times and then she and her spear back out of the box.

I can hear something out there, but I can't quite place the sound, and when I scoot my bottom out of the box, she's sitting on the riverbank with her face buried in her sleeve, crying.

I kind of bob around in front of her, trying to figure out what to do. She looks up and spits out, "Now I'm gonna have to move!"

I sit next to her and say, "No, you're not! We won't tell anyone."

She snickers, "Oh, right. You tracked me all the way out here and you're not going to tell anyone? Give me a break! I give it two days. Cops'll be swarming this place and next thing you know I'll be back in a foster home wishing I was dead."

"I swear I won't tell anyone! I don't think you should have to live out here, but..."

She jumps up. "See? This always happens! Someone comes along and tries to *help* me. Why can't people just leave me alone?" She kicks the dirt and says, "Living out here's a whole lot better than living in some foster home or under the bridge with those derelicts."

"Derelicts?"

"Yeah. Those bums don't have anything better to do than swipe your stuff or hit on you." She flashes a look at me and says, "This place was perfect. Why couldn't you just have left me alone?"

I push sand around with the toe of my high-top a minute. "You don't have to move. Really. I'll swear Marissa and Dot to secrecy and..."

She just rolls her eyes. "Yeah, right. We'll see how long

that lasts." She looks at the box and says, "It was a lot of work. It's the best one I've had."

I try to sound real casual when I ask, "How many have you had?"

She scowls at me. "You're awfully nosy, you know that?" Then she looks off over the riverbed and says, "About four."

I'm staring at her, thinking about everything she's said, when she turns to me and sighs. "I ran away in June." And suddenly she's not looking like the Riverbed Savage anymore. She's looking scared and lonely and tired.

"Why?"

She hurls a rock into the sand. "I'd rather live like this than be locked in a closet or made to eat *dog* food." She throws another rock and says, "I'm also not into having my head dunked in the toilet."

My eyes must've been bugged way out because she laughs and says, "I guess you've never been Sani-flushed, huh?"

I just shake my head.

"Why you working at the soup kitchen anyway? You some kind of nun-in-training or something?"

Well, that's a laugh. "No! I'm working off a detention for school. I've got twenty hours to do and my Grams arranged for me to work it off at St. Mary's."

"Twenty hours? Wow. The most I ever got was two."

"So where'd you go to school?"

She scowls at me. "There you go again. It's none of your business and I'm not gonna tell you. Next thing you know you'll be calling up my old school and getting me thrown in another stupid foster home. Just back off, okay? I'm doing fine. In another few years I'll be able to get a job and get on with life. Right now I just want to be left alone."

I take a deep breath. "What are you going to do when it rains?"

"Get wet—what do you think?" She stands up and says, "I'll survive, okay? And now if you don't mind, teatime's over."

I start up the bank and then I remember her backpack. I turn around and say, "Look, Holly, if you did take the goblets and cross, at least give back the cross. It's Father Mayhew's and it means a lot to him."

"Like I said, you're no different than the rest of them."

I take a deep breath and say, "Well, you haven't actually said you *didn't* take them. And I'm not asking because you're homeless. I'm asking because the day Father Mayhew's cross got stolen I saw you leaving the church, and yesterday I heard something clinking around in your backpack. Sounded like goblets to me."

"So I'm a suspect, just for going to church, huh?" She whips her backpack from behind a bush and pulls out two old horseshoes. She clinks them together and says, "And you think *these* sound like gold? Don't I wish! I took them to the Thrift Store, but CeCe wouldn't give me a nickel for them." She hurls them out to the riverbed. "Fat lot of luck they've brought me!"

Now watching those rusty horseshoes skid into the sand, I feel bad. Really bad. For the way she lives, for what she's been through. For ever having suspected her. But all I can seem to say is, "I'm sorry."

She shakes her spear at me and says, "Talk to your friends. I don't feel like moving, and if one of you rats on me..."

I say, "Trust me, no one's going to rat on you."

"*Trust* you? What a laugh." She shakes her head and snickers. "Haven't you figured it out yet? You can't trust anyone."

"But I trusted *you*. I told you all kinds of top-secret stuff!"

"Well, I guess you're not too bright, then, are you?"

I walk up the bank, but as I turn to look back at her, I don't see the Riverbed Savage that she wants me to see. I see a skinny girl in jeans and a sweatshirt, trying to act tough while she's shaking in her high-tops.

I duck back through the bushes, and as I'm stomping across the field, I think about rain and wind and winter. And when I get to the sidewalk, I look back at the path cutting through the weeds. And I want to run back and drag her out of the riverbed and into a house, because there's no way she's going to make it through the winter in that refrigerator box.

No way.

TEN

Every time I tried to think about something else, my brain would find a way back to Holly. I thought about her sleeping with her spear at night and about her eating cold spaghetti for breakfast. I thought about her having to wait for the sun to come up to go pee in the bushes and how long it must take to warm up in the morning. Mostly, though, I thought about all the people who must have betrayed her and how the last thing I wanted was to become one of them.

I couldn't exactly call Marissa and Dot on the telephone and make them swear not to tell anyone about Holly—not with Grams right there in the apartment. So when school rolled around on Monday, I'd practically forgotten about the softball tournament; all I could think about was getting Marissa and Dot to swear to secrecy.

I didn't have a chance to get them alone until lunch, and by then Marissa was so wrapped up in preparing for the game that when I asked her to swear, all she said was, "Right, right, sure," and went back to talking about softball.

Dot, though, interrupts her and says, "I thought we'd already decided not to tell anyone. Why are you so worried about it?"

"I'm not worried. Holly is."

They both look at me and say, *"Holly?"*

So I tell them about my trip out to the riverbed. And I'm just getting to the part where Holly practically runs me through with a whaling knife when I notice Monet Jarlsberg coming our way.

Now, I don't let Monet know I've spotted her. I just unwrap my peanut butter and jelly sandwich and whisper, "Whatever you do, don't turn around. Heather's little scout is coming this way and I have a feeling it's not to buy us sodas."

Marissa and Dot do a lot of twitching in their seats, but they make themselves not turn around. And when Monet slides onto the bench right behind them, we all get real busy eating our lunches and saying stuff like, "I can't believe Mr. Tiller gave us forty-five problems for homework tonight," and "What are you going to do for Thanksgiving?"

In between chewing and talking about nothing Marissa and Dot are bugging their eyes way out, mouthing stuff like, "Where is she?" and "What do you want to *do*?" and I'm bugging my eyes right back at them mouthing, "Shh! Shh! Right behind you!"

And I'm right in the middle of getting the bright idea that we could be giving Monet some *wrong* information to take back to Heather, when she stands up, "accidentally" elbows Marissa in the head, and says, "Oh, I'm sorry! Gee, I hope that didn't hurt!" Then she says, "Well, if it isn't the B Team!" like she's so surprised to find us sitting there.

Marissa and Dot just kind of shake her off, but I look

straight at her and smile. That's all—just smile. And she starts to leave, but before you know it, she's back at our table saying, "Don't give me that stupid little smile, Sammy. You guys are so deluded. The whole school knows you're gonna get slaughtered today. Even your outfield wants to bail."

I'm about to say something like, So why are you wasting time snooping on us? but *Marissa* smiles at her and says, "They can bail if they want. You guys aren't going to be hitting any balls out there anyway."

Now you have to understand—Marissa doesn't usually stand up for herself. She kind of lets people take advantage of her and then feels bad about it for the rest of the day. So when she puts Monet down and then takes a bite of hamburger and smiles at her like, Try me, girl, Monet doesn't quite know what hit her.

Marissa puts a hand up for us to slap, and Monet huffs off. And when we're all done yipping, "Yes!" and giving Marissa high-fives, she wipes her mouth and says, "We are going to win today," and for the first time I actually believe her.

Since the game was scheduled for the last hour and a half of school, we only had one more class before the teams got to go suit up. And by the time we were all clomping around in our cleats, the rest of the school was down at the diamond, getting yelled at by Mr. Caan to back up and sit down.

Aside from being our vice principal and the one who's got me working at St. Mary's, Mr. Caan is also our home plate umpire. And since he hovers right behind me when

I'm catching, I try not to let too many wild pitches get past me.

While Mr. Vince huddles up in the infield with his team, Ms. Rothhammer and Miss Pitt holler at us to take a long lap and then circle up out in left field. Miss Pitt is a student teacher this year, which means she's practicing to be a teacher. Some days she just sits and watches Ms. Rothhammer, but lately she's been running the class more and more and Ms. Rothhammer's been watching *her*.

Anyhow, when we're circled up, Miss Pitt calls, "Count 'em out! Loud!" so we all start yelling, "One...two...three...hey! Two...two...three...hey!" as we do our jumping jacks.

And while our team's busy yelling numbers at each other, Mr. Vince is huddled up with his team, probably going over strategy and last-minute signal changes.

Mr. Vince always does real complicated signals. He'll slap himself all over really fast—first one arm, then the other, then a leg, then his head and his neck and his thigh—and while he's busy playing himself like a bongo drum, you're supposed to remember that it's the signal after he slaps, say, his stomach that counts.

He also does really gross signals. He'll stand in the coach's box with his finger up his nose—or scratch his butt or hock a loogie—and that's supposed to *mean* something. Trouble is, Mr. Vince is always picking his nose or scratching his butt or hocking loogies, so half the time his team doesn't pick up the signals, and then everyone gets to watch him yell his head off and dance around the coach's box like a bug on a barbecue.

Anyhow, Ms. Rothhammer goes off to do the toss while we finish stretching, and when she comes back she says, "We're in the field, girls." She hugs her clipboard and says, "Remember, back each other up, and *visualize* winning. Forget about the crowd, forget about looking good. If you play good, you'll look good, and the only way that's going to happen is if you concentrate on the game, not the people watching you." She bites the inside of her cheek a minute. "I know you can knock the socks off Mr. Vince's team, and ladies...nothing would give me greater pleasure."

We all look at each other sideways, because Ms. Rothhammer's always even-tempered and in control, and you can tell—she's a little hot under the jersey about one eighth-grade history teacher.

So while we're busy pulling faces at each other, Miss Pitt puts her hand out and says, "C'mon, girls, show 'em who's number one!"

We all pile our hands on top of hers and yell, "Go! Fight! *Win!*" and then race off to the bench to get our gear.

For everyone else "gear" is a glove and maybe a ball to warm up with. For me it's a mountain of padding and a mask. I've got to put on a chest protector and shin protectors, and by the time I've wrestled into my mask I look more like a porky potato bug than a girl.

After I'm dressed, I always go off by myself for a minute and, well, kind of talk to my mitt. It's not like I say, Hiya, Mitt! How's it going? It's more like I go over the signals out loud or tell myself I'm going to have a good game.

And when I'm all done talking, I count the loops in the laces and tug on the knots, and just spend a minute with my mitt.

And my dad.

Anyhow, I'm in the middle of counting loops when I hear Marissa call, "Sammy! Warm me up! C'mon, it's time!" and sure enough, everyone's in position but me.

So I crouch down behind the plate and hold out my glove, and after a few practice pitches Mr. Caan signals Mr. Troxell to take his position umpiring in the field.

Mr. Troxell's the boys' P.E. teacher. He's big and boxy and really tan, and his hair's buzzed right down to his scalp. When he's in position, Mr. Caan steps behind me, flips down his umpire's mask, and calls, "Batter up!"

From all the whistling that's going on I can tell without looking that it's Julie Jaffers stepping up to bat. She's tall and blond, and she's got curves that could show through a catcher's shell.

She *doesn't* catch, she plays first base, and she's good. Actually, she's great. She's left-handed, which means she catches with her right hand, and with her being so tall she can snag a ball *miles* away from first without ever leaving the bag. The last thing you want to do if Julie Jaffers is on first is slap a ball down the first-base line. She'll snap it up like a frog snags a fly, and you'll be out before you can say, Rats!

Anyway, I check the fielders, and everyone seems ready, so I crouch, flash Marissa the signal for a curve, and put up my mitt. Marissa presents the ball, then squints and windmills the first pitch. It comes sailing in like it's going to nail Julie in the stomach, and then curves right over the plate.

I throw the ball back to Marissa while Mr. Caan yells, "Steeerike one!" and jams a finger up in the air.

Julie slaps the plate with her bat and then holds it real still, high in the air by her left ear and waits.

I signal Marissa for another curve, put up her target, and *whoosh*, there it comes, straight for Julie's stomach and then over the plate.

"Steeerike two!" yells Mr. Caan and jams two fingers in the air.

You can hear people yelling, "C'mon, Julie!" and you can tell from the way she's slapping the plate that she's not about to get suckered by another curve. I set up my mitt low and inside, and when Julie swings at the pitch she does it like she's expecting it to curve out. She connects with the ball all right, only she does it way down the handle of the bat and all the ball does is dribble straight out to Marissa. Julie doesn't even run to first. She takes three steps and then shakes her head and goes back to the bench while Marissa scoops up the ball and tosses it to Xandi Chapan.

Miss Pitt is going a little crazy jumping up and down, yipping, "Way to go, girls! One up, one down! Keep it up, keep it up!"

Then Gisa Kranz comes up to bat. Gisa is a foreign-exchange student from Germany. And even though she speaks pretty good English, when she gets excited or mad—which is pretty often—her words come out in German. And even when she's not excited or mad, "yes" comes out *ja,* and "that" comes out *das.* You can always tell when someone's been talking to Gisa 'cause *they'll* say *ja* and *das* for a few sentences instead of yes and that. I guess it's kind of contagious.

Anyhow, Gisa plays third, and when she's in the field you can hear her yelling, "Ja!" or, "Is mine!" or just yelling at the ump. If there's one thing I know about Gisa Kranz, it's that she's definitely not shy.

I also know that when she's at bat, she'll swing at the first pitch. Every time.

So when she whacks the bat against the plate, digs in real good, and calls out to Marissa, "*Ja,* let's have it, girl— I'm ready!" I signal Marissa to throw a riser and then set up her target.

And sure enough, Gisa swings and pops a fly ball right out to Dawn Wilson at shortstop. Dawn catches it for an easy out and halfway to first Gisa starts sputtering in German. Nobody could tell you exactly what she was saying, but let me tell you, the meaning was loud and clear.

So while Gisa heads back to the bench, Miss Pitt goes into hyper-hop, yelling, "Way to go girls! Two up, two down. One more time!"

Now usually you're not lucky enough to have three up and three down. One of the first three batters usually slips by. But we had two up and two down, and that put Heather in danger of being the third out, which is worse than you might think. See, if you're the first out, or even the second, well, *you'll* remember you made an out, but chances are other people won't. What they *will* remember is that So-and-So made the third out. It's almost like if

94

you make the third out, you're responsible for all of them. It's not fair, and people would tell you it's not even true, but trust me—I've been the third out lots of times and that's the way it works.

So here's Heather, a seventh grader up after two eighth graders have just gone down, and what's she thinking? That there's no way she's going to shoulder the third out. She slaps the plate, gives me the Evil Eye, then waves her bat in the air like she's going to lasso a cow.

When I give the signal for a curveball, Marissa just stands firm on the mound and shakes me off. Now, this has only happened a couple of times before, and both times what she wanted was to pitch a fastball, straight down the middle. So I set up her target, but very slowly Marissa leans her head back—she wants the target higher.

Up goes my mitt a tad, and in comes the pitch. Heather swings all right, only she just gets a piece of it. The ball pops up and back, so I flip off my mask and dive to catch it. When I dig myself out of the dirt, there's the ball, smiling up at me from my mitt, and there's Heather, glaring down at me like she's going to kill me.

I just dust off and try to ignore her. Mr. Caan steps over and says, "Move along, Heather," because he knows that Heather's on the verge of slicing and dicing.

So I yank off my armor and join the rest of the team at the bench, and when Miss Pitt gets done dancing around telling us what a great job we did, Ms. Rothhammer looks at her clipboard and says, "Okay, you know the batting order: Dot, Sammy, Xandi, then Becky, Marissa, Kris,

Dawn, Cindy, and Jennifer. Remember, whether you're on the bench or warming up, focus on the game. Try to pick up Mr. Vince's signals, look for weaknesses...stay sharp. What you pick up while you're waiting for your turn at bat can be as valuable as a good play in the field. Keep your eyes open!"

While the rest of the team lines up on the bench, Dot and I pick through the bats until we each find one that feels good. And while I'm on deck loosening up a bit, I hear Babs Filarski say through her catcher's mask, "Little Dotty's up to bat. Eeeeeeasy out."

Now, that's just not true. Dot's a good hitter. Babs is just one of those psych-out catchers. She'll harass you into swinging, and do stuff like snicker or laugh when you're about to lean into a pitch. And if the umpire's standing far enough back she'll call you things that would make Mr. *Vince* blush. If you don't get a decent pitch early on, you stop caring about whacking the ball and start thinking about whacking Babs.

Anyway, Dot just scowls at her and then Mr. Caan straightens out his face protector and calls, "Batter up!"

So Dot gets up, taps the plate a few times with the end of her bat, then raises it and waits. And waits and waits some more. And the other team's pitcher, Emiko Lee, never does present the ball. You can see her out there, flipping it around and around in her glove, and finally she steps off the mound and calls, "I need a new ball."

Mr. Caan straightens out and says, "That *is* a new ball!"

Emiko just shakes her head. "It's lopsided!"

Mr. Caan pushes back his mask and walks out to the

mound, but before he's even halfway there, Mr. Vince is next to Emiko, taking over, inspecting the ball. The three of them stand out there for a while, arguing, and while everyone's busy waiting, Ms. Rothhammer sneaks over from the third-base coach's box and says to Dot, "It's a psych-out, Dot, just relax. Close your eyes and picture yourself slamming that ball right past Gisa clear out to Anita and beyond. You can do it. Just stay cool."

Mr. Caan gives Emiko another ball, and after she does a few more warm-up pitches she digs herself a good toe-hold, presents the ball, and then windmills a pitch right over the plate.

And Dot whacks the stitches off it. It goes smashing past third and out to left field just like Ms. Rothhammer told her to. She takes off like a firecracker, shooting around first and straight at Monet Jarlsberg on second. And when she sees Anita Arellano hurling the ball to Monet, she pours it on and then slides in, hooking the corner of the bag with her toe.

When the dust dies down, she's safe and Babs Filarski is steaming like a teapot. She kicks some imaginary dirt off home plate with her cleats and when she sees me waiting for her to back up, she practically spits, "Uppity seventh graders." She straightens out her chest protector and it looks like she's about to shove me, when Mr. Caan calls, "Let's go, girls. We haven't got all day."

The first pitch Emiko throws is low and outside. Way low. And as it's coming in Babs says, "Swing!"

I don't. I step back and then measure up for the next pitch.

It comes in low and outside again, and Babs calls, "Swing!" *again*.

I almost did. I mean, I *want* to hit the ball. I've got all this adrenaline pumping and I want to run, not walk. So when the third pitch comes, Babs doesn't have to tell me to swing. I watch the ball sail straight in the strike zone and *wham!* I whack it with all my might.

Trouble is, the pitch was a riser, and before my bat even hit the ground I knew I was out. I tore off down the baseline anyway, because Ms. Rothhammer's always yelling at us to give it the gun even if it looks hopeless, but I wasn't paying much attention to first base—I was watching the ball take a nice little stroll through the air, straight for shortstop, straight for Heather Acosta.

Heather lines up right beneath it, all right. Then she looks my way and drops it. That's right, the giveaway pop-up of the season and she drops it. She scoops it up and fires it to first, but it's too late. She's just given me a freebie and let me tell you, I'm taking it. And as Xandi Chapan comes up to bat, there's Heather across the field, glaring at me like it's *my* fault she dropped the ball.

I blow her a kiss and get ready to lead off. And when the ball leaves Emiko's hand I move out about ten feet, keeping one eye on Dot and the other on Xandi. When Xandi swings, she misses, so I scoot back to the base and so does Dot.

We wind up doing that two more times. On the third strike, Xandi throws down the bat, spins on Babs, and yells, "Shut up, would you?"

Now, even through all her gear you can tell that Babs is

smiling. And as Becky Bork steps up to the plate, Babs crouches into position and calls, "One out, force at second or third!" because she's expecting to pick off two more outs without chipping a nail.

What she wasn't expecting was for Becky to bat left-handed. See, Becky's right-handed, but sometimes she decides to bat the other way. And, right or left, she doesn't just hit grounders. Ms. Rothhammer's got her fourth in the lineup because if Becky connects with the ball, it's *gone*, and that usually means we're on the board.

Trouble is, that's a big if. Becky's gone *games* without connecting, but it doesn't seem to bother her. She just comes back to the bench with, "I'll get it next time. Wait and see. I will."

So Becky picks the heaviest bat available, steps up, and slams the plate a few times like she's trying to crack it open. Then she tucks in her lower lip and wags the bat in the air.

Emiko plays with her toehold a bit, then whips a pitch straight through the strike zone.

Becky keeps on wagging.

Mr. Caan yells, "Steeerike one!" and Babs tosses the ball back to Emiko.

Emiko plays with the ball a minute and then whips another one right down the middle.

Becky keeps right on wagging.

Now, I'm looking at Dot and Dot's looking at me, and we're both getting kind of nervous. I mean, Becky's up there looking like a crazed robot waving a wooden arm, and we're both thinking there's no way she's going to get a hit, let alone drive us in.

Then Emiko does something she should never have done. She throws her a change-up. Against any other power hitter a change-up might've been a good idea, but against Becky? Mis-take! That's *her* pitch.

The minute Becky sees that ball coming toward her, well, the crazed robot with the wagging wooden arm comes alive. She steps into the pitch and *wham!* It goes hurling out to right field, and no amount of praying is going to land that ball in Tenille Toolee's glove.

So around the bases we go, just kind of dancing across home plate and giving each other high-fives until our hands hurt.

And when the cheering finally dies down and Dot, Becky, and I are back on the bench, I look out at the field, and I can't see much but Heather. She's out there, pacing between third and second like a caged tiger. A hungry caged tiger.

And I can tell from the way she's looking at me—I'm her pail of meat.

ELEVEN

We won, 6–1. Mr. Vince's team did make some good plays, and I hate to admit it, but Heather made two terrific outs. But I think they were so thrown by the first inning and we were so charged by it that they kept blowing it, and the mistakes we made just seemed to wash right off.

For a while we thought we might even shut them out, but then Gisa hit a ball clear over Kris Zilli's head, and before you know it, Gisa's dancing up and down on home plate yelling, "*Ja! Ja! Ja!* I did it! I did it!" and they were on the board.

After the last out, we tried to go up and shake hands, but they just ignored us. All except Heather and Emiko, that is. Heather gave me the scariest Evil Eye I've ever seen, and Emiko went up to Marissa and told her, "Great pitching. You deserved the win."

So while their team is getting yelled at by Mr. Vince, Miss Pitt waltzes around giving us hugs, saying how proud she is of us. We're all keeping half an eye on Ms. Rothhammer, though, because she's in the enemy camp with her hand out to Mr. Vince.

At first he stands there like he's much too busy holding a clipboard to shake her hand, but finally he shuffles things around and gives her a quick shake. And when Ms. Rothhammer jogs back over to us, there's a smile dying to explode all over her face.

She stands there for a minute, studying her tennis shoes. Then she looks up and says, "You girls did me proud," and if I didn't know her better, I'd swear there were tears in her eyes. "I'll talk with you individually tomorrow, but right now I want you to go over and shake hands with Mr. Vince's team."

Xandi says, "But we already tried!"

Becky chimes in with, "Yeah, they snubbed us."

Ms. Rothhammer gives us a wise little smile. "I know that. Try again. Try harder." We stand around looking at each other until she claps her hands and says, "C'mon, girls. Move it!"

Mr. Vince's team tries to ignore us again, but Mr. Troxell makes them line up. We come through and shake hands, mumbling, "Good game," back and forth, and then there I am, cleat to cleat with Heather Acosta. And I'm looking straight in the eyes of someone who'd shove me down the shaft of an outhouse without blinking, but for some reason I'm not feeling scared or mad or spiteful. I'm feeling bad that we're such enemies. And I find myself wondering *why* she hates me so much. I mean, sure, I've called her Turd-face and Eggbreath and I've trespassed on her property a time or two, but she hated me way before that. And really, what I've done to her is nothing compared to what she's done to me.

But standing there, I wished that it would all just go away. That I could walk around school not worrying about what plan Heather's concocting to embarrass me. That we could both just live in our own little pockets of the world and forget about each other.

So I take a deep breath, put my hand out, and say, "Good game, Heather," and in my heart I know—I mean it.

And what does she do? She spits on me. *Splat,* right in my face.

Now, that's too much, even for Mr. Vince. While everyone else is sucking in air and covering their mouths, he yanks her out of line and drags her off for a good talking-to.

Dot and Marissa huddle in and say, "I don't *believe* it!" and you can tell that Dot's dying to tackle Heather and choke the saliva out of her.

Ms. Rothhammer calls, "Let's go girls, back to the locker room!" but the three of us stay put while I wipe spit off my face. And it's funny. I'm still not feeling scared or mad or wanting to get back like I would've even a few hours ago. What I'm feeling is sorry. Not for myself. No, for the first time in my life, I'm feeling sorry for Heather Acosta.

* * *

The last thing I felt like doing was putting in my two hours at St. Mary's. I wanted to hang out with Dot and Marissa and talk about the game! And it wasn't until we were about halfway to the mall that I started thinking that maybe I could do both. "Hey! You guys want to come help me stuff envelopes for the Sisters of Mercy?"

Dot says, "What are you talking about?"

"I've got to help Sister Bernice mail out fliers for their shows. C'mon! It'll be fun."

They look at each other and shrug. Marissa says, "They won't care?"

"Heck, no!"

When we get to the mall, Dot calls her mom, and then we're off to the church to find Sister Bernice.

I spot Father Mayhew walking along the parish hall with Gregory, so I run up to him and say, "Father Mayhew! Have you seen Sister Bernice?"

He smiles at me and says, "Afternoon, lass," and right away, Gregory tries to give me his carrot.

I scratch him behind the ears and say, "No, thanks, boy," but somehow I wind up with this slobbery carrot in my hand and Gregory in front of me, wagging and panting.

Father Mayhew laughs and says, "Toss it for him, lass. It's all right."

So I toss it, and as Gregory goes charging off to retrieve it, I look around for someplace to wipe my hand. Father Mayhew says, "I believe the Sisters are in their motor home—right over by the parish hall."

Before I've had a chance to clean off my hand, Gregory's back trying to get me to throw it again. I try to ignore him, and say to Father Mayhew, "I brought a couple of friends to help. You don't mind, do you?"

Father Mayhew smiles and waves at Marissa and Dot, standing a little ways down the sidewalk. "I'm sure the Sisters will be delighted."

Well, there's that carrot stump in my hand again, only this time it's got a big goopy strand of slobber on it which runs between my fingers and onto the back of my hand. I throw the stupid carrot and try wiping the slobber off on the grass, but all that really does is coat my hand with grass clippings.

Father Mayhew says, "I'm sorry about that, lass," but I don't want to stand there and discuss it while ol' Bunny Breath digs his stump out of the bushes. I just say, "That's okay," then hightail my tarred and turfed hand back to Marissa and Dot.

The three of us go charging over to the parish hall, but kind of sputter to a stop when we see the Sisters of Mercy's motor home.

I don't know how I'd never noticed it before. The thing's like a whale on wheels. It's white with purple stripes going around it, and propped over the parish hall lawn is an awning that could shade half a beach. And sitting in a lawn chair with a cellular phone to her ear is Sister Bernice.

She gives us a great big smile, holds up a finger, and says into the phone, "Wonderful. I'll look forward to meeting you at ten…um-hm, you, too. God bless," and then punches the OFF button.

She motions us closer. "Sammy! What's this? Has our Good Shepherd brought me a flock?"

"If it's okay with you."

She laughs and says, "It's more than okay! We've got so much to do before Thursday, I've got to laugh to keep from crying." She gathers some papers from a table. "In this business, timing is everything, and unfortunately, everything has to happen all at once." She smiles and looks off at the sky and sings, "But I...yi yi, I'm a believer," and even in the wide-open spaces of the parish hall lawn her voice sounds big and full and powerful.

She grins at us. "So, my little lambs, let's get you stuffin' and stampin'."

We follow her to the motor-home door, only she turns around and says, "Wait right here, okay? We'll be doing this at the parish hall, I just need to get the supplies."

I say, "Um, Sister Bernice? You know Father Mayhew's dog?"

She laughs, "Ol' Growler-yowler? Why, sure."

"Well, he made me throw his carrot and—"

"He made you throw his carrot? You got that close to him?"

I laugh and say, "Yeah. For some reason he likes me." I hold up my hand. "Anyhow, it was really slobbery and I'd like to wash this, if you wouldn't mind?"

She stands at the base of the steps and frowns for a minute, looking at my hand. Then she breaks into a smile and says, "Well, that certainly could use a little soap and water." She pulls a key from the sleeve of her habit and brings her voice way down when she says, "My Sisters like the solace of their own quarters, so try not to disturb them, okay?"

I nod, so she unlocks the door and steps inside.

Now, I'd never been inside a motor home before. Not even a little one. And I wasn't expecting to see what I saw. There was a living room—an actual living room, with couches and a coffee table and a television. And the furniture was all this kind of puffy velour with a soft pink and white pattern like the sky in the background of an oil painting.

To the left of the living room was a dining room booth, and across from that was the kitchen. And I'm talking *kitchen*. Four-burner stove, refrigerator, microwave, overhead cabinets—the works. And humming away in the kitchen, placing vegetables from the refrigerator into the sink, is Sister Clarice.

So I'm checking all this out when Sister Abigail calls, "Bernie, I've got those faxes sent. Do you—" She sees me and says, "Well, what have we here?" only she's kind of glaring at Sister Bernice and I can tell that I'm intruding.

Bernice says, "You remember Sammy, don't you?"

I hurry up and say, "I'm sorry, I just need to wash my hands before we start stuffing envelopes."

Abby flips down the screen of a computer, shuts off the power to a printer, and comes up from the passenger seat. "They don't have a basin at the hall?"

Bernice says, "Lighten up a little, Sister. Sammy's not the one that tried to break in the other night. She just wants to wash her hands."

Clarice smiles at me from over at the sink. "Nice to see you again, Sammy. I'll be done here in just a minute. Why don't you have a seat?"

Now, I don't want to sit on one of the couches—they look too puffy for someone with dog slobber on her hands. So I sit on the edge of the dining room booth and watch Clarice. She shakes the water off a freshly washed beet and carrot and puts them in a blender, tops and all. She adds a bowl of papaya slices, then cracks an egg on top of them, but instead of putting the shell in the garbage, she puts it in the blender, too. Then she covers the whole mess with pineapple juice, puts on the lid and *vrooom!* She whips it up.

And in about thirty seconds she's got this pink drink that looks more like a strawberry milk shake than a compost concoction. She holds up the pitcher. "Would you like a taste?"

I smile and shake my head, but she pours a little in a glass anyway and says, "Go on, it's *good*."

Well, what am I supposed to do? I watch her take a big gulp from her own glass, and since nothing happens to her, I pick up mine with my clean hand and take a sip.

And it doesn't taste anything like weeds and beets. It's *good*. So I say, "Hey, that's amazing!"

Sister Clarice pulls a face at Bernice and Abby. "Told you so."

Bernice laughs and says to Abigail, "Lord, have mercy, she's a brave one." She takes the glass from me and swishes the drink around. "Sister's been trying to get us to try this all week." She raises the glass in the air and says, "May the Lord protect and keep me," then downs the drink, smacks her lips, and says, "Aah!" Her eyes pop wide open. "Say, that *is* good!"

After Abigail finally breaks down and tastes it, Clarice clears out the sink and says, "It's all yours, Sammy."

While I'm scrubbing up, Abigail goes back to the front of the motor home, Clarice sits in the living room to finish her drink, and Bernice ducks into the bathroom. When I'm done, I grab a paper towel from the roll and dry my hands, and when I look around, well, there's no trash can. So I pop open the cabinet under the sink because that's where everyone keeps their trash can, only there isn't one—just pipes and soap and scrub brushes. I start to open another cabinet, only Clarice jumps up and says, "Right over here, dear," and holds out a wastebasket.

I throw out the paper towel and stand around for a minute, but without Bernice there, I feel really awkward so I go to the door and say, "I'll just wait for Sister Bernice outside."

Marissa and Dot are sitting on the lawn, and when they see me coming, Dot says, "What took so long? Where's Sister Bernice?"

"Sorry. Sister Clarice was cleaning vegetables in the sink. I had to wait."

Marissa hitches her thumb at the NunMobile and says, "My uncle has one of those. They're amazing. The kitchen table turns into a bed, and there's a loft above the driver's seat. There are compartments everywhere— even under the benches and the furniture. My uncle's has a TV in it, too—right between the front seats. It is so cool."

Just then Bernice comes walking down the steps with a big box. "You angels ready to help in the service of the Lord?"

We follow her over to the parish hall, and when we push through the front door, who do we see? Brother Phil sitting at a table with his face in his hands. And near him, back against the wall, are Father Mayhew, Sister Josephine, and Mary Margaret.

And we stop cold, because across the table from Phil is Officer Borsch.

You can tell from the way Officer Borsch is pacing back and forth that he's not there discussing the merits of using a crosswalk. He's there to beat a confession out of Brother Phil.

When Officer Borsch sees me standing in the doorway, he stops pacing and sits down. And for a second it looks like *he's* going to bury his face in his hands, but he doesn't. He just sighs and says to Father Mayhew, "We're not getting anywhere." He wags his head over at us. "And now we've got company. Maybe we should go down to the station."

Father Mayhew shakes his head. "The station? Is that really necessary?" He takes a step closer and says to Phil, "Son, you swear you didn't take the chalices or the cross, but you have no explanation as to why you were going through the drawers in the sacristy this afternoon. What am I supposed to think?"

Phil shoves back from the table. "You want to know why? I'll tell you why! Thanks to you, I'll probably never be ordained. Thanks to you, I..." He closes his eyes tight, and says real slowly, "I just wanted to try on the vestments. I just wanted to see what it felt like."

Father Mayhew runs his complicated eyes over him a minute. Then he says as gently as he can, "Son, you're just not ready. Maybe someday you will be, but you're not now. And if what you say is true, wanting to play dress-up in a priest's clothing just serves to convince me that you have a lot of work to do before your ordination."

After a minute of nobody saying anything, Officer

Borsch and Father Mayhew go out one door and the Sisters and Brother Phil go out another. After they're gone, Sister Bernice shakes her head a bit and mumbles, "There's bitter blood running through this place." She gives us a half-hearted smile. "We've got a lot of work to do ourselves, girls. Let's get to it."

She sets up a little assembly line for us and when she's sure we know what we're doing, she says, "Just bring 'em along to the motor home when you're done. And girls? Keep in mind that the Lord works in mysterious ways. He'll find a way to help my Brothers and Sisters exorcise whatever demons possess them. Have faith."

After she leaves, we stuff envelopes for a little while without saying much, but pretty soon Marissa and Dot are back to talking about the game and how we're going to shut out Mr. Vince's team on Wednesday.

I'm talking about it, too, only part of my brain's not thinking about softball. It's tingling and twitching, brooding about Brothers and Sisters. And it seems that the more I get to know the Family of St. Mary's Church, the harder it is for me to tell which ones are the saints.

And which ones are sinners.

TWELVE

Sometime between us stuffing envelopes and me serving sandwiches at the soup kitchen, I guess God decided the church needed a good washing. At first I thought it was going to be the usual move-along-a-little-faster kind of rain, but it wasn't. It was a downpour.

About halfway into serving sandwiches, people started cramming into the soup kitchen, wanting to eat their food inside. But there isn't very much room, and Mary Margaret finally had to say, "I'm sorry, but you're going to have to move along. We just don't have the facilities to shelter you."

So they shuffled back outside, and most of them just disappeared—probably over to the mall to dry out a bit. But you could see a handful of them hanging out under a tree, putting newspapers across their strollers and carts, trying to keep all their stuff dry.

And just as I'm thinking that we're done for the day, Holly comes dripping in. Her hair's matted flat against her head, her sweatshirt's soaked clear through, and her high-tops squish when she walks.

Now, if this had been Marissa or Dot, I would've taken one look and started cracking up. I mean, she looks like a wet whippet ready to shake out and soak the walls.

But she's not Marissa or Dot, and she can't just shake herself dry. And I don't laugh. I don't even smile. I just whisper, "You want me to try to get you some dry clothes?"

She takes her sandwich. "It's just water." Then she turns and whispers over her shoulder, "Don't get any bright ideas. I'm fine."

Well, I don't *have* any bright ideas. I want to tell *someone* about Holly, but looking around, well, Josephine's a Sister and all, but she doesn't seem too sisterly. And Mary Margaret's nice, but she'd wind up doing the same thing Father Mayhew would do if I told him: call the police. And in no time they'd haul Holly back to civilization where she'd be nice and warm on the outside, and miserable on the inside.

So I didn't tell them. I just headed home in the rain. And when I got past Mrs. Graybill and popped into the apartment, the first thing Grams says is, "Oh, thank heavens! I was getting worried."

I almost told Grams right then and there, but she waves me straight into the bathroom. "Go on, Samantha—get out of those clothes! You're going to catch your death of cold."

So I went into the bathroom, and standing there in front of the mirror, dripping, well, *I* looked like a wet whippet in squeaky high-tops needing to take a good shake all over the walls. After staring at myself for a minute, I wrestled out of my backpack and checked to make sure my mitt hadn't gotten wet, then I peeled off my clothes and jumped in the shower.

That night I dreamt about softball. Only it wasn't a regular softball game—we were playing in the pouring rain. And when it was my turn to bat, instead of Anita, Debbie, and Tenille being the outfield, it's the Sisters of Mercy, and they're in habits and cleats, waving their gloves in the air, singing, "Take me...take me to the river...Wash me...wash me in the water..."

*   *   *

It rained all night. And by the time I was ready to leave for school, it was *still* raining, so when Grams hands me her big old black umbrella, I take it. I fly down the fire-escape stairs like Mary Poppins from a rooftop, cut across Broadway to Maynard's Market, run all the way down to Cook Street, and before you know it, I'm sloshing my way up the school steps.

In homeroom the kids take one look at my umbrella and start teasing me, saying, "What is that thing? A tent?" because it's big enough to keep a gorilla dry. I just laugh and put it against the wall next to all their collapsible jobbies, and in between classes, I stay nice and dry while their umbrellas turn inside out in the wind.

It finally quit raining around lunchtime, but the patio tables were too soggy to eat at so we all wound up piling into the cafeteria. Between classes kids would yell through the rain, "You were awesome yesterday, Marissa!" and she'd smile and wave, "Thanks!" But at lunch, she got mobbed. All the seventh graders wanted to tell her what a great pitcher she was and how she was going to be the first seventh-grade pitcher ever to win the Junior Sluggers'

Cup and how she'd go down in the Softball Hall of Fame and stuff like that. She was being real nice about it, saying it was a team effort and everyone played well, but you could tell that she was happy to be the star.

Then, when Danny Urbanski came over and sat with us, well, I thought Marissa was going to pop. Danny's cute, but to Marissa, being near him's like being on a runaway train. Her hands shake and her heart races and she thinks she's going to die. And I swear, if he's even halfway nice to her, she picks me off the ground and twirls me through the air.

Danny was being more than halfway nice to her. He was joking around and telling her what a great pitcher she was, and the whole time he's talking, he's playing with the silver ring he wears on his index finger.

When he leaves, Dot whispers, "Who was *that*?" and for the first time in days, Marissa went on and on about something besides softball.

I think Heather ditched school that day. Maybe she didn't come because she was sick, or maybe she had a family emergency out of town, but I doubt it, because Tenille wasn't at school either. Tenille'll do anything Heather says, and I don't know—them both being gone made me a little nervous. I could just see them, locked up in Heather's room, bouncing around on Heather's bed, smoking cigarettes and plotting ways to chop me into little pieces.

Don't get me wrong—I had a great day without Heather. People were friendly to us all day long, and when school let out, the sun was actually shining so we had a really nice walk home. Well, over to the church, anyway.

I don't think Marissa and Dot were planning to stay, but Sister Bernice must've seen us, because she comes charging out of the NunMobile with a bundle of bright purple fliers and cuts across the lawn.

She's not wearing cleats, but she's *moving*. The lawn's pretty soggy from all the rain, and you can see water splashing from under her habit as she calls, "Girls, you're here! Oh, the Mighty One has answered my prayers! Thanks be to God!"

And you'd think from the way she was carrying on that the NunMobile was on fire and we had a hose, but all she wanted was for us to plaster the neighborhood with fliers. "As far and wide as these'll take you," she says. Then she shoos us off with, "Go on, lambs! Time's a-wasting!"

So we paper the neighborhood purple. And when we're rid of every last flier, I'm late getting to the soup kitchen and Marissa and Dot are late getting home.

When Brother Phil opens the back door for me, he doesn't smile and say hello. All he says is, "You're late," like he's *paying* me or something.

I say, "Sorry. I was putting up fliers for the Sisters of Mercy."

Sister Josephine hears that and mutters, "Figures," so I say, "I don't get it. Why don't you like them? Aren't they doing all this work to raise money for St. Mary's and the soup kitchen?"

She laughs, but it sounds more like a backfiring car. "They get fifteen percent of the money that's donated. They're not in service to God—they're out for themselves! Sister and I can't even afford to *rent* one of those motor homes for a week to go on vacation, let alone buy one." She thumps her cane on the floor and says, "'Sisters of Mercy'...hah!"

Now, I'm thinking that if the Sisters of Mercy take fifteen percent, that leaves the church with eighty-five percent, which, considering all the work Bernice and the others are doing, is quite a lot. But I don't say that to Sister Josephine. I just go over to the serving line to relieve Sister Mary Margaret.

Mary Margaret says, "Oh, hi, dear," so I ask her, "Have any young people come through already?"

"A few children. Is that what you mean?"

"Uh, no. I meant someone more my age."

Mary Margaret's face lights up a bit. "Oh, her. No, she hasn't been through today." Then she whispers, "Do you know her?"

I shake my head. "I was just wondering."

Sister Mary Margaret gives my shoulder a squeeze and says, "We can only be there for them and try to guide them. The rest we must turn over to God."

I get to work passing out food, only my brain's not doing a very good job of turning Holly over to God. And the later it gets, the more often I check the door to see if she's waiting in line.

When there are no more people, Brother Phil says, "That's it. Let's clean up."

Normally, that would've been fine with me, but since there were still a few sandwiches left, I said, "Can we give it another few minutes?"

Phil snorts, "You can if you want to." He grabs a

117

sandwich and says over his shoulder, "Me, I'm ready for a snack."

He leaves, so I duck under the table and peek out the door, and after I check up and down the street a few times, I make myself accept the fact that Holly's not coming.

I go back inside, and as I'm moving the trays to the sink, I'm wondering if maybe she got sick or hurt or...or I don't know what. And as I'm putting the leftover milks back in the refrigerator, I get a great idea: if Holly can't come to the soup kitchen, maybe the soup kitchen can come to Holly. I stuff two sandwiches and a carton of milk in my backpack, grab my umbrella, and head off to the riverbank.

By the time I make it to the bushes I'm soaked from the knees down from walking through soggy weeds. And I'm thinking about that refrigerator box holding up in weather like this. A Hefty bag might be good for garbage, but a roof? And besides, it didn't go *underneath* the box, and if the rain seeped in from the riverbed, well, cardboard in water lasts about as long as a graham cracker in the tub.

And I was so busy thinking about Holly's poor house that I about jumped into tumbleweeds when I heard a voice. A man's voice. And then, when I heard him laugh, let me tell you, I shivered. That laugh was *evil*.

Very quietly I peel off my backpack and set it down, then I grab the umbrella and sneak down the hill.

What I see is Mr. Tattoos from the soup kitchen. He's got both of Holly's wrists in one hand and her down sleeping bag in the other. Holly's kicking and yelling,

"Give it back! Give it back!" but she's not getting anywhere, and the harder she tries, the harder he laughs.

I go charging down the hill and he hears me coming, but not soon enough. I ram him in the back with the point of Grams' umbrella and he lets go of Holly, but doesn't go down.

He screams, "Oooooww!" and then cusses his head off while he's hobbling back toward the box with one hand on his back. "There's *two* of you brats?"

Holly says, "Yeah, there're two of us. Now give it back!" She lunges for her sleeping bag and the next thing you know, Tattoohead stumbles and falls through the box like an axe through oatmeal.

Holly cries, "No!" but it's too late. Her house is ruined. And he's all tangled up in Hefty bags and tumbleweeds, trying to cuss his way out, when Holly snatches her sleeping bag. Trouble is it catches on the branch of a tumbleweed and feathers go flying everywhere. So she's standing there holding one end of her ripped-up bag, and he grabs the other and yanks as hard as he can. More feathers go flying in the air and before we can even scream, Holly's bed is in shreds on the ground.

Holly scoops up her sleeping bag, crying, "No... no...*no!*"

He laughs and says, "That should teach you, you flea-bitten brat," and takes off down the riverbed.

I go over to her and say, "Oh, Holly."

She plops down in the wet sand, buries her face in her hands, and starts crying. And pretty soon she's shaking from crying so hard, so I sit next to her, put my arm around her, and say, "I'm so sorry," because I don't know what else to say.

Finally, she shakes her head and says, "What am I going to do? What am I going to *do*?" And sitting there on the soggy riverbank with her shivering in my arms, all of a sudden I had an idea. And the more I thought about it, the more I talked myself into thinking it was a good idea.

A very good idea.

THIRTEEN

The whole time we were walking Holly only said about two words. I think she was thinking about her sleeping bag, and how in the world she was ever going to replace it. I know she wasn't thinking about spending the night at the Pup Parlor, because as I push on the buzzer, she looks through the window and says, "You want me to sleep in a *kennel?*"

I laugh. "It's not a kennel. It's a place where they groom dogs. But look—there are rooms upstairs."

She steps back and looks up while I lean on the buzzer some more, thinking, "C'mon, Vera…c'mon!" because if she's not there, I don't know what I'm going to do.

Now, I would've told Holly about how nice Meg and Vera are and how they're always taking in stray dogs so of course they'll take her in, only I'm not sure. I can just hear Meg saying, Sammy, a stray girl is *not* a stray dog! and then what?

So my brain's busy scrambling around for a backup plan when Vera comes pattering down the stairs in her bathrobe and slippers. She squints at me through the glass. "Sammy! What brings you here at this hour?" She looks us up and down and asks, "Is it an emergency?"

"Kind of. Can we come in?"

She tightens her robe and says, "Sure. Would you like to come up? It's a bit chilly down here."

I say, "Thanks," because it *is* cold, especially in soggy clothes.

When we get upstairs, Meg calls, "Who was it, Ma?" then turns around from a sink full of dishes and says, "Sammy?" like she can't quite believe I'm there again.

"Hi, Meg. Do you have a minute? There's something I have to talk to you guys about." She doesn't budge from her sink of suds so I look straight at her and say, "It's important."

Vera takes us into the living room, and the whole time she's sizing up Holly. When we're all sitting in chairs, Vera disappears a minute and then comes back with a floor heater. She doesn't say a word, she just plugs it in and puts it at Holly's feet.

Holly leans over it, rubbing her hands together. "Thanks."

Vera and Meg both look at me like, "Well?" so I take a deep breath and say, "This is Holly. She's a friend of mine and she needs a place to stay. I was thinking maybe you could work something out where she works in the shop and you give her room and board." Then, before they can jump up and say no, I say real fast, "You've had that HELP WANTED sign up forever..."

They don't say, Sure, let me tell you. They don't say anything. They just check Holly over. Then Meg says, "But she's a minor. There's laws against doin' that!"

I say, "Look, she doesn't have anywhere else to go. She's been living out at the riverbed in a refrigerator box, but tonight this man with tattoos came and ripped up her sleeping bag and destroyed her box."

Meg's eyes pop right open and she says to Holly, "You've been *what?*" and Vera sits straight up in her chair and says, "He did *what?*"

I whisper to Holly, "Tell them. Just tell them!"

Holly looks back and forth between them and then looks down at her hands. "I ran away from this foster home I was stuck in. They promised me it'd be better than the last one, but it wasn't. Instead of throwing me in the basement, they'd lock me in a closet. Instead of whacking me with a broom, they'd use a mop....It was the same thing all over again."

Meg's eyebrow is arched way up, and she's busy eyeing Vera, trying to get her attention. And at first I thought she was thinking, How could someone do that to her?! but then I realize that what she's thinking is that there's no way she's taking in a girl that's so wild you have to lock her up in a basement.

I say, "Wait! It's not what you think. These people stuck her head in the toilet and flushed it. They made her eat dog food. It's not that Holly's bad—they were just mean."

Vera and Meg sit there with their mouths hanging open, and finally Holly let's out a stuttery little sigh. "I've been in about eight foster homes, and they've always been the same. None of them wanted me—they wanted the money. So when I was big enough, I ran away."

Meg starts pacing around, throwing her hands through the air, saying, "The Richters have foster children—

they've taken them in for years. They're saints! So have the Montonyos. Their house is immaculate and their children are happy and loved. You make it sound like foster parents are just in this for the money, but I know for a fact that's not so!"

Holly looks down and you can tell that she's about to cry. So I jump up and say, "Maybe it's like dog kennels—you know, some of them treat the dogs real nice and others, well, you pick your dog up and it smells like pee and it's hacking with kennel cough and scratching from fleas. Maybe it's like that, and Holly just happened to get stuck in some rotten...uh...kennels."

Now, the minute it's out of my mouth I'm thinking, Boy, was that stupid, but it seems to calm Meg down and she looks at Holly like, Hmm.

Vera says, "Holly, dear? Where are your parents?"

Holly shakes her head and shrugs. "They're dead."

We all look at her and wait, so she says, "I don't even remember them, okay? All I remember is being bounced around from home to home. It's not like I've ever even *had* a family." She looks out the window. "I don't blame you for not wanting to help me out. And believe me, I don't really *want* your help. I just want to be old enough to be on my own."

Very gently, Vera asks, "How old *are* you, dear?"

Holly keeps staring out the window. "Fifteen."

Now, there's no way she's fifteen. No way. And Vera knows it, too. She says, "The truth, dear. If we're going to talk about this at all, you need to tell us the truth."

Holly looks at her, and then back out the window. She

sighs and says, "Okay, so I'm only fourteen." She checks back, and when she sees that it's not washing she chokes out, "I'm twelve," and starts to cry.

Vera and Meg look at each other, thinking, What are we going to *do?* while Holly's soaking the sleeve of her soggy sweatshirt, wiping tears off her face. And just as I'm thinking someone's got to say *something,* out from under a chair comes the tiniest dog I'd ever seen. It's like a cross between a chihuahua and a miniature poodle, and there's no mistaking it—this dog belongs to Meg and Vera. It's got black fur, and on either side of its little poofball-do are little red bows. At first I thought it was going to go sit in Vera's lap, but instead it goes over to Holly, jumps up in her lap, puts its paws on her chest, and licks away her tears.

Holly gives it a hug, then lets out a little laugh and says, "Hi, there," as she pets it. She looks at Vera and says, "What's her name?"

"Lucy." She laughs. "Or Miss Lucille, when she's being naughty."

Holly gives the dog another hug. "Hi, Lucy."

The rain was coming down again, hitting the window like a shower of nails. Vera gets up and says to Meg, "Let's talk about this in private."

So Holly and I sit there for the longest time, not saying much. And watching Holly with Lucy, well, she doesn't seem at all like the girl who about ran me through with her whaling spear. She seems like a nice, normal girl. Finally, I ask, "Do dogs always take to you like this?"

She sighs. "Dogs are the best."

"You're going to love it here, then."

She puts Lucy down on the floor. "They don't want me to stay here. You know it and I know it, and it doesn't really matter." She stands up and says in kind of a tough voice, "I'm gonna get going....Thanks anyway."

Before I can say, Wait! Vera and Meg come back into the room. Vera says, "Don't run off, dear, we want to talk to you."

Holly kind of eyes me and you can tell—she's afraid to hear what they have to say. But Lucy comes up and nuzzles her leg, so Holly picks her up and sits back down.

Meg says, "You can stay under these conditions—" but Vera interrupts with, "What Meg's trying to say, dear, is that we'd like to try having you stay with us, but there're some things we're a little worried about."

Holly hugs Lucy a little tighter. "Like?"

Meg says, "Like breaking the law. I don't want to get into a lot of hot water for taking you in, and I don't think it's fair for you to spend what's left of your childhood working in the shop." She takes a deep breath. "We have a spare room that you could use. We'd give you your meals, and you'd work downstairs with us three or four days a week...after school."

Holly's eyes pop wide open. "School? But—"

Meg says, "No buts about it. You go to school or the deal is off."

Very slowly, Holly nods.

Vera sighs and says, "What we haven't figured out yet is what we're going to do about registering you at school. But we'll think of something." She smiles at Holly. "So what do you say, dear? This ain't the presidential palace,

126

but at least you'll be warm and comfortable. And you have my word—we'll never lock you in the closet."

Holly lets out a long, choppy sigh. "I won't be any trouble, I swear." And when she gives Lucy another hug, she doesn't look suspicious or angry or scared.

For the first time since I met her, Holly Janquell looks almost happy.

FOURTEEN

We were in the middle of homeroom when Holly showed up. The office lady, Mrs. Tweeter, walks her in, says a few words to Mrs. Ambler while she gives her Holly's add slip, then disappears.

Holly looks just the same, only drier and cleaner. And she's standing up there like every kid that's ever been stuck in a new school in the middle of the year, kind of looking at no one and hugging her binder like she's afraid it's going to fall.

I want to call out, "Hi, Holly!" but I'm way across the room and I don't know if that's going to make her feel better or worse.

After a minute of Mrs. Ambler talking privately to her, she puts her arm around Holly and says, "Class, this is Holly. She comes to us from Albuquerque, New Mexico. I know you'll make her feel welcome." Then she looks around and says, "Let's see.... There's a seat, right behind Heather." She smiles at Heather. "Maybe you could help Holly out with her schedule and introduce her to a few friends."

Heather smiles back at Mrs. Ambler, but what she's thinking as she's checking Holly out is there's no way she's going to help out a kid in high-tops. And sure enough, when the dismissal bell rings, Heather jets off without a word.

I go up to Holly and say, "I can't believe you're here already!"

Holly shakes her head. "Me neither. I think they were up all night plotting their strategy."

"But you like it there okay?"

She shrugs and says, "We'll see how long it lasts. French toast for breakfast, though, and Lucy gets to sleep with me." She looks down and toes the ground. "Uh, Sammy?"

"Yeah?"

"Thanks."

I smile. "Sure. I hope it works out." I look at her schedule and say, "Classes today are really short 'cause of the softball game."

"What softball game?"

"The last hour and a half of school everyone goes out to the field to watch the playoffs. You'll see." I hand her schedule back and say, "We've got three classes together, so don't worry about getting confused. I'll help you. Right now we'd better get over to English and listen to Miss Pilson read to us in a foreign language."

She gives me kind of a puzzled look, but after we're in English listening to Miss Pilson read Shakespeare, she grins at me because she knows *exactly* what I'm talking about.

At lunch Holly sat out at the patio tables with us and pretty much just listened to us talk about the game and what the field was going to be like after all that rain. When the bell rings, she says, "Good luck today, you guys," and you can tell that she really is excited for us to win.

When game time finally rolls around, Dot, Marissa, and I zip off to our own little corner of the locker room, and we're pretty happy, whispering and giggling about how we're going to win. Then, while Marissa and Dot fix their hair, I run off to the bathroom. And I'm not gone for more than two minutes, but when I get back my mitt is not where I left it.

At first I think they're playing a joke on me. I mean, they're right there, you know? Who's going to run up and steal my mitt with them standing there? So I say, "All right, you guys, give it back."

Marissa looks at me through the mirror. "Give what back?"

"Ha, ha. Very funny. Now, give it back."

They both turn around. "Give *what* back?"

Well, looking at their faces, I can see they don't have a clue what I'm talking about. So I look under the bench and inside my locker, and then I run back to the bathroom and check, even though I know I didn't take it with me.

When I come back, I say, "It was right here on the bench with yours. What could've...?" Then I see Tenille and Heather huddled up in a corner, looking like they've just snuck in the EXIT doors at the movies.

I go up to Heather and say, "Hey, that's really not cool—give it back."

She snickers and says, "Since when do *you* know anything about being cool?" She tightens the laces of her cleats. "Besides, I don't even know what you're talking about."

My heart's beating pretty fast, and I'm dying to throw

her against the lockers, but I just stand there and try one more time. "Heather, you're not going to win the game by stealing my mitt. Now, c'mon. I know you've got it, just give it back and let's play each other fair and square."

She gives me a sour little smile. "'Play each other fair and square, play each other fair and square.' Isn't that just like you, you little cheater." She puts on her glove, punches it with her fist, and says, "Good luck, Sammy. You're gonna need it," then turns her back on me.

I march straight up to the phys. ed. office. And when I tell Ms. Rothhammer what's happened, she says, "Are you sure?"

"I'm sure."

She grabs her keys and comes flying down the steps into the locker room, then corners Heather and says, "I'd like you to open your locker for me. Right now."

By now all the eighth graders have figured out that something's going on and they're all huddled up in pockets, whispering to each other. But since they can't figure out exactly what's happened until they break down and ask a seventh grader, they just watch while Heather goes over to her locker and pops it open.

Heather says, "See? I don't have it. She's just trying to get me in trouble again."

Ms. Rothhammer mutters, "Yeah, like the way she forced you to spit on her after the last game." Then, without missing a beat, she turns to Tenille and says, "Open your locker."

Panic whitewashes Tenille's face. She stutters, "Ms. Rothhammer, I...I don't have it—really!"

131

Ms. Rothhammer puts her hands on her hips. "Open it. Now!"

So we go over to Tenille's locker, and while she's flipping the combination around, I see the eighth graders on our team break down and wave Marissa and Dot over so they can find out what's going on. So the rest of my team's in one corner of the locker room and I'm with Ms. Rothhammer in another, and when Tenille finally gets her locker open, all Ms. Rothhammer finds is some dirty socks and a pack of cigarettes.

She takes the cigarettes and says to Tenille, "I'll deal with you about these later." She turns to the rest of the players and says, "I want this locker room turned upside down. You know what Sammy's mitt looks like. Find it!"

My team does just that, but Heather's team only pretends to look. And after ten minutes of us finding nothing, Ms. Rothhammer comes back with one of the school's gloves. "This is the best I can do, Sammy. I'm sorry. We've got to get out there—we're already late."

Now, the glove isn't a catcher's mitt. It isn't even a first-baseman's mitt. It's a glove that barely covers my fingers. And running out to the field with the rest of the team, I'm thinking that I'd be better off bare-handed.

Miss Pitt tries to fire us up during warm-ups, but Marissa's pretty worried and I'm really upset, and I guess it's kind of contagious, because we can hear Mr. Vince's team count off better than we can hear ourselves.

We're up first, and while Dot's getting in some warm-up swings, I try getting used to the glove I've got to use. But the more I work it, the more it feels like I've got a porcupine stuck in my throat, and hard as I try, I can't keep my eyes from dripping.

Then the strangest thing happens. It's like a flash going through my brain. I see Father Mayhew staring out the window of his office, crying. And all at once I know, way down inside, how he feels about his cross being stolen.

I stay there for a few more minutes, sniffing and dripping, but pretty soon Dot's in the batter's box and I've got to get on deck, so I swallow the porcupine, hurl the mitt under the bench, and head out.

The crowd's sounding like a giant Morse code machine, chanting, "Dot-Dot-Dot!" and even though she swings at the first pitch and misses, she practically cracks the bat slamming out a line drive on the second one. But it's a line drive straight to Gisa Kranz, and even though Dot flies over to first, she's out.

When I get up to bat, I eye Babs Filarski's mitt and I guess she knows I'm thinking maybe I can borrow it, because she snorts, "Dream on!"

I didn't even connect. When Babs called, "Swing!" I swung, and before I knew it, it was Xandi's turn to bat and I was back riding pine.

And after Xandi struck out, well, it was basically all over. No one seemed to be able to hit, and when we were in the field, I couldn't catch, I couldn't throw—I could barely remember the signals. In the last inning Heather drove in the final run and we got shut out, 5–0.

Afterward, Mr. Vince's team was more than happy to shake our hands, and Heather was more than happy to sneer at me and say, "Good game!"

I didn't spit on her, but let me tell you, I wasn't standing there feeling sorry for her, either. I was mad. Mad at her for taking the one thing that made me feel like somewhere I really *did* have a dad, and mad at myself for not being able to play without it. And standing there watching her sneer at me, I knew—she and Tenille had ditched a whole day of school so they could figure out a way to get me to blow the game.

I looked her straight in the eye and said, "Maybe you won the game, Heather, but anyone who'd steal someone else's mitt is a loser. A big loser."

She thinks that's pretty funny. She throws her head back and laughs, "*I'm* a loser?" and pretty soon her whole team's laughing and nudging each other, and by the time we're back in the locker room that porcupine's back and no amount of swallowing is making it go away.

On the walk home Marissa's going on and on about how embarrassing the game was, and when she says, "Did you hear him out there? 'Go, Marissa! C'mon, Marissa!'— Danny was actually cheering for me and I couldn't hit the broad side of a barn!" I yell, "Stop it! Just stop it! The whole thing's my fault. You know it, I know it, the whole team knows it! I'm sorry, okay?"

Marissa shuts up for a second and Dot says, "C'mon, Sammy. It wasn't your fault. Everybody made mistakes."

I look at her and just shake my head because no matter what she said, no matter what anybody said, it wasn't going to change the fact that I'd let Heather get to me.

Get to me big time.

FIFTEEN

Marissa turned off to play video games at the mall, and Dot decided she had to go straight home, so I just rested on the curb outside St. Mary's for a few minutes before going inside.

St. Mary's is a big church. A really big church. If you count the parish hall and the priest's quarters, it takes up a whole square block. The church has a tower that goes up about six stories, and on the very tippy-top, looking like it's trying to snag the clouds, is a big brass cross.

And sitting on the curb looking up, I see a big purple and white banner flapping against the tower that reads HAVE MERCY! Then the KSMY Roving Reporter Newsvan comes whipping past me and I can see Zelda Quinn scribbling like crazy on a notepad.

If you've ever been to Santa Martina and turned on the news, you know who Zelda Quinn is. She's the only newscaster on the planet with a skunk-do. It's puffy and black—all except for this white streak that goes from above her right eye clear over the top of her head and down the back of her neck.

So when I saw the skunk-do streaking down Church Street, I knew that Zelda Quinn had been to St. Mary's to get the scoop on the Sisters of Mercy. And when I turned up the church walkway, instead of the usual list of Mass times, the marquee read:

Experience the World-Famous
SISTERS *of* MERCY
in a
GOSPEL CONCERT
THU, FRI & SAT—7 PM
$15 Cash Donation

Taped to the front door of the church are posters of the Sisters of Mercy singing and dancing, in their habits and in costumes, and on a table right inside the church is a stack of fliers like the ones Dot, Marissa, and I plastered all over the neighborhood.

So between the banner flapping on the tower, the marquee, the posters, and the fliers, there's no way you could be anywhere near St. Mary's and not know something big was going on.

And I was just wondering how I could get my hands on a ticket when I hear music blasting out of the church. I'm not talking organ music, or even piano. I'm talking drums and electric guitar—*loud* music.

I go through the foyer and there's Sister Bernice up at the altar with two giant speakers and the biggest boom box I've ever seen, saying, "Check! Check!" into a microphone.

Sister Abigail is on the far end of the church and she waves at Bernice to shut off the music. "Boost the lows, cut the mids, and roll off a bit of the high end. And try angling the speakers out some. The slap-back's awful back here!"

Bernice plays with the boom box and speakers for a minute and then calls, "Ready?"

Abigail nods and up comes the music again. She moves from one end of the church to the other, then up close and far away. After a minute Bernice starts singing into one mike and Clarice goes back and forth between two other mikes, singing a harmony part, and *wow*—they were good!

When they were all done with their sound check, Bernice waves to me and calls, "Sammy, angel! Am I glad to see you!" She hurries down the aisle and says, "Are you handy with an iron?"

Before I can answer, she whisks me down a hall to a room at the back of the church, and there, hanging from cabinet knobs and closet doors are costumes. Bright, *wild* costumes.

And as I'm standing there with my mouth gaping open, trying to picture the Sisters of Mercy rocking out in feathers and sequins and purple satin, Bernice grabs the skirt of a gown and says, "Most of these are all right, but some of them need a touch-up." One side of her mouth tries to smile, but the other just stays put. "At most parishes the other Sisters help us out, but here—well, God's given us a real challenge. Would you mind, lamb?"

Just then Father Mayhew walks in, looking a little flustered. He smiles and says, "Samantha! Oh, good. Will you be helping the Sisters out?"

I say, "Sure," even though the last time I tried ironing

something it was for my mother, and as far I know, some of Lady Lana's blouse is still on her iron.

But I set up and get to work. At first I'm pretty slow. Instead of steam, the water's coming out in little puddles, and all I'm doing is making the clothes look wet and blotchy. But after a couple of skirts I start to get the hang of it, and pretty soon I'm slapping that iron around like I've been doing it all my life.

While I'm working I'm not thinking about *fabric*. I'm thinking about the game. And the more thinking I do about the game, the faster I iron, and pretty soon I'm in my own little cloud of steam, not noticing I've got company.

I don't know how long she'd been watching me, but when I looked up and saw Josephine standing in the doorway I about branded the ceiling.

"I figured they'd shanghaied you into doing their dirty work," she says. Then she thumps her cane on the floor. "Sister Mary Margaret's come down with the flu. We really need you over at the kitchen...if you don't *mind*."

Now I'm not about to argue with her—not with the way her cane's starting to wobble and all. I just unplug the iron and follow her over to the soup kitchen.

Right after we get there, Brother Phil blows in all out of breath. And while his stomach's pumping in and out like a giant bellows, he plasters his hair back in place and says, "I walked in on him going through my room at the seminary! Can you believe that?"

Sister Josephine whips around and says, "Mayhew? You caught Father Mayhew going through your room?"

Phil says, "The Holy Highness himself. I walked in on

him tearing apart my closet. Can he just do that? Isn't there a law or something?"

Sister Josephine thinks about this a minute, then scowls and says, "Probably not. The seminary *is* church property." She looks at him sideways, "Well? Did he find anything?"

"I tell you, I didn't take it! Any of it!"

Sister Josephine just shrugs like, If you say so...

Phil turns pink as a petunia. "What—what are you saying?"

Just then someone rattles the door really loud. Sister Josephine and Brother Phil keep right on staring each other down, but I look up at the clock and see that we're late. So while Phil and Josephine are busy spitting insults at each other, I go over to the refrigerator and pull food and drinks out until all that's left is the lightbulb. Then I set everything up and prop open the door, and when I look back across the room, Phil is going off in a huff out one door, and Josephine's going off in a huff out another.

I wound up running the whole show by myself, and actually, it was easy. No one tried to steal extra food, and the one thing I was kind of worried about—Mr. Tattoo coming through—never happened. I just passed out food until all the people were gone, then I popped the leftovers back in the refrigerator, punched the knob lock, and closed the door.

On the way home, I stopped by Hudson's. I went up on the porch and could see him through the living room window, watching TV. He waves me inside and who's he checking out on the TV? The Sisters of Mercy, rockin' and rollin' at St. Mary's altar.

And it's kind of strange, seeing them on television. It's almost like watching some crazy rock video instead of the news. Then the camera turns away from the altar and focuses on Santa Martina's very own Skunk Reporter.

Zelda shouts over the music, "It promises to be some show, and for a good cause. Performances are at 7:00 P.M. Thursday, Friday, and Saturday at St. Mary's Church." She smiles and says, "Zelda Quinn, KSMY News."

Hudson shuts off the TV. "Aren't those nuns dynamic? St. Mary's has needed something like this for years." He tugs one of his bushy eyebrows and says, "Well, I'm convinced. I'm going." Then he winks at me and says, "And I'm taking your grandmother with me, whether she wants to go or not."

I'm busy picturing Grams at the show with her chin down to her chest and her hands over her ears, when Hudson says, "What's troubling you?"

I blink at him. "Um, I was just thinking that maybe Grams wouldn't be the best company at the show because..."

He shakes his head and says, "Out with it. Your aura's dim, and if I know you, it's got to be something big to have you this down."

"My *aura*? What are you talking about?"

He frowns. "Your energy glow. It's almost completely gone. Now, out with it, Sammy."

So I sigh and sit down. And once I start, I can't seem to stop. I tell him about the softball tournament and my mitt and Heather, and how empty I feel inside. And then I tell him about Father Mayhew and his cross, and how upset

I'd been that he'd accused me, but that now I understand a lot better why he did it.

Hudson nods, but he looks very serious and he doesn't say a word.

Finally, I ask, "Hudson?"

"Hmm."

"What are you thinking?"

He eyes me and says, "That you're the lucky one."

"Lucky? Me?"

He nods again. "At least you know whom to distrust. Not knowing your enemy makes you jump at the sight of your own shadow. It makes for a very unnerving existence."

Well, if there was one thing I *hadn't* thought of myself as being, it was lucky. But I sat there imagining not having a clue who had taken my mitt, and he was right — that would be worse.

"Father Mayhew has no idea who stole his cross?"

"Well, he used to think it was me, and I used to think it was Holly, but now I think he thinks it's Brother Phil."

Hudson puts up a hand. "Whoa, whoa. Back up a bit, Sammy! Obviously you're above reproach, but who is Holly, and why did you think she took it?"

So I wound up telling him all about Holly coming through the soup ktchen and how we followed her to the riverbank and found out about her cardboard house and all of that. And the more I tell him about Holly, the higher his eyebrows creep up, and when I'm all done, he lets out a long, low whistle and says, "That's some story!" Then he nods. "Asking Meg and Vera was a stroke of genius. Obviously, they're a godsend for her, but she'll also be good for the two of them. As much as I enjoy Rommel, dogs do not a family make."

I think about Holly being part of the Pup Parlor family and laugh. "As long as they don't start doing her hair!"

He laughs, too, then smooths down an eyebrow and says, "So how'd Holly do at school today? That had to be quite an adjustment for her."

Now, to tell you the truth, I'd forgotten all about Holly after my mitt got stolen. I'd spent all my time thinking about Heather and the game and how mad I was at myself. So all of a sudden I felt terrible. I mean, it isn't easy being in school even when you have friends. Starting seventh grade when you *don't* has got to be like walking through the mall in your underwear.

I put my hand in front of my mouth. "Oh, no! I should've waited for her after school!"

Hudson studies me. "Why don't you go over and see her now? I'll call your grandmother and tell her where you are."

"Well…um…maybe *I* should call Grams."

His eyebrows creep toward each other like albino caterpillars. "She *does* know about all this, doesn't she?"

I give him a guilty grin. "Not exactly…"

He shakes his head. "She needs to know what's going on with you. Otherwise she worries."

"She worries either way. I just think she worries less *not* knowing."

Hudson's caterpillars are practically smooching. "She needs to know, Sammy. It's all over now, so you don't mind if I tell her, do you?"

I shrug, "Go ahead, I guess. Just tell her not to tell anyone else. I don't want people to get all nosy and then have Meg and Vera decide she can't stay with them anymore. Holly'd just run away again."

Hudson nods, and while I'm strapping on my backpack, he gives me a little smile. "It's coming back already."

"What's coming back?"

"Your aura. It's already brighter."

I laugh and say, "Oh, my *aura*," and wave good-bye.

And as I'm walking to the Pup Parlor, I tell myself that Hudson's right about me being lucky. At least I know which one of the glasses on my table has poison in it. Poor Father Mayhew has to go thirsty because it could be in any one of the glasses on his.

Or maybe, just maybe, there's a little poison in all of them.

SIXTEEN

The sign said CLOSED, but I could see Meg and Holly through the window, sweeping up. And I was just about to lean on the buzzer when I noticed that they weren't just sweeping. They were also laughing and singing along with the radio.

Now, even though the only times I'd been with Holly she'd been either about to kill me or scared to death, it didn't seem strange seeing her laughing and singing. It just seemed like Holly doing something she *should* be doing.

Meg, on the other hand, I've known for a long time, and even though she's usually friendly, she always seems sort of tired. You know, beat down. So seeing her be-bopping around with her little bows and broom, well, it seemed kind of strange. Like she was a different person. A happy person.

Holly notices me gawking at them through the window and lets me in. "Hi, Sammy!"

I smile and say, "Hi, Holly...Hi, Meg."

Meg dumps the last of the dog hair in the garbage, then smiles at me and says, "Nice of you to stop by. Vera's up fixing lasagna. Can you stay?"

Lasagna sounds great, but I know I should be getting home to Grams. "Thanks, but no. I just came over to ask

Holly if she wants me to come by on my way to school to-morrow." I look at Holly. "We could walk over together if you want."

Holly says, "That'd be great!"

"So how'd it go today? I'm sorry I didn't look for you after school. I was, uh...well, I was kind of preoccupied."

Holly puts away her broom. "What happened, anyway? Everyone was saying you really trounced them the first game."

The last thing I want is to start talking about the game again, so I just shake my head and say, "It's a long story. I'll tell you about it on the way to school tomorrow if you really want to know." Then I wave and say, "Bye! See you in the morning," and head out the door.

Grams was still on the phone to Hudson when I got home. And when she got off, she sat down and just looked at me. I said, "I'm sorry I didn't tell you about Holly earlier," but she just kind of waved it off and said, "No, no, that's okay." And for the rest of the night she was really *quiet*—like she wanted to be left alone with her thoughts.

We both wound up going to bed early, and when I fell asleep, I had another softball dream, only this time when I got up to bat the Sisters of Mercy weren't in the outfield. Bernice was catching, Abby was on second, and Clarice was on the mound. Clarice kept pulling balls out of her habit, only they weren't really softballs—they were giant marshmallows. And when I'd swing the bat and connect, the marshmallow wouldn't go anywhere. It would just stick to the end of my bat like a giant wad of glue.

145

And while Abby jumped up and down on second yelling, "Cut some mids! Cut some mids! We need more balls out here!" Bernice held out this way oversized catcher's mitt, calling, "Ball!" for every pitch so I *wouldn't* swing and she could catch the ball and eat it.

*   *   *

The next morning when I showed up at the Pup Parlor, there's Holly, all ready to go. And at first I thought it was going to be really fun, having someone to walk to school with. She tells me all about Vera and Meg and how nice they're being to her, and then she asks me about the game. So I tell her about Heather and my mitt, and she seems really interested, asking me all sorts of questions. But when we turn off Broadway, she quits looking at me and starts eyeing trash cans instead.

That's right. Trash cans. All the way down the street there are trash cans on the curb, waiting to be collected. And every time we walk by one, Holly kind of looks inside and checks out what's there.

At first I'd kind of slow down and wait for her, but after a while I just kept on walking, hoping that she'd keep up with me and quit checking out everyone's garbage.

It didn't work. She'd snoop through a trash can and call out, "So why do you think she's the one that took your mitt?" or "Why does she hate you so much?" which are kind of hard questions to answer anyway, even when you're not watching someone snoop through garbage.

Then she stops in front of this one house and starts *digging* through the trash. She's up to her elbows in dump

146

filler and I just can't take it anymore. I throw my hands in the air and say, "What are you *doing?*"

She pops up with this old plastic sea-foam green purse and says, "Check it out!" like she's just reeled in a ten-pound trout.

"Holly, what are you *doing?* That's someone's garbage!"

By now she's snapped the purse open and is checking out the sea-foam lining and all the little sea-foam compartments. And when she finds a pair of matching gloves in one of the pouches she squeals, "Wow! Look at these! I don't think they were ever even worn!"

Now, I'm standing there, thinking, Gee, I wonder why, when she snaps it all back together and says, "CeCe'll buy this off me. No doubt about it." She holds it up in front of me. "What do you think? Three bucks?"

I haven't got a clue how much CeCe would give her for a sea-foam purse with matching gloves, and I'm looking around because we're pretty close to school and the last thing I want is for someone like *Heather* to see me inspecting thrift-shop gems from a garbage can. So when Holly says, "Four bucks?" I practically yell at her, "I don't know! Why are you doing this? You're not homeless anymore—you don't have to dig through garbage anymore! Why are you doing this?"

Now, it sounded really mean, and right after I said it I was sorry. She gets real quiet and says, "It's not garbage. It's just stuff people don't want anymore." So we walk past a few more houses and I'm trying to figure out how to say I'm sorry when she stops at another trash can and says, "You'd be amazed at what people throw away... Here, look at this," and pulls up a Teddy bear with an amputated leg.

I whisper, "Holly!" like I'm afraid someone's going to hear me talking to this trash hound.

She dives right back in and comes out with the leg. She pieces them together, then looks at me and says, "See? He's a fine bear. Someone was just too lazy to sew him back together."

I cover my face with my hands. "Holly, it's *garbage*. Put it back!"

She goes back into the trash can, saying, "Wait! Wait! I know I saw some.... Here it is!" and pops back out with a red-and-green plaid ribbon. She whips it around little Teddy's neck and ties it in a bow. "There. Now he's a Christmas bear!"

I have to admit, there's nothing about the bear that a needle and thread won't fix, and he actually *is* looking pretty cute, but I'm still checking over my shoulder for Heather Acosta and I can't quite get *into* it, if you know what I mean.

Holly gathers her bear and her bag and off we go. And as we're getting closer to school, I'm starting to wonder how she's going to survive being the new kid at school with a sea-foam purse and a broken bear, when all of a sudden she ditches them both behind a bush and says, "They'll be safe there 'til after school, don't you think?"

I let out a big sigh of relief. "They'll be fine."

She laughs at me. "You didn't think I was going to take them into *school*, did you?"

148

I shrug and say, "I didn't know!"

"What do you think I am...crazy?"

We both laugh, and just as I'm feeling a little better, it hits me where I am. I'm at the place where I'd completely embarrassed myself the day before. The place where a wicked beast with red hair stalked me and thirsted for my blood. I'm at school.

You may think I'm exaggerating, but as I'm walking up the steps I hear, "Oh, look! It's the poor little kitten!"

I turn, and there's Heather and all her little friends, pointing and laughing.

Heather sings, "Poor little kitten has lost her mitten and she can only cry, 'Ms. Rothy-dear, see here, see here, my mitten I have lost!' 'What? Lost your mitten? You *loser* kitten! Guess you shall have no pie!' Meow, meow, meow-meow-meow!" And while she's doing the meow part, all her little wannabe friends join in and sing, "Meow-meow-meow!" which just makes Heather sing the whole thing again, only this time louder.

Holly tugs on my sleeve and whispers, "Let's get out of here!"

We go through the administration building because I know Heather won't follow me in there, and as we make it out the other side, Holly shakes her head and says, "That girl is vicious. What's her deal?"

I shrug and say, "I don't know. I guess she really wants to win." But as we cut over to homeroom I get a little revelation: Winning's important to Heather, all right.

But it's not nearly as important as seeing me lose.

SEVENTEEN

Marissa came into homeroom right as the tardy bell rang. I could see her across the room, all flustered and out of breath, but when she looked over at me, she was smiling. Happy smiling. I mouthed, "What's going on?" as we saluted the flag, but she just winked and patted her backpack.

When Mrs. Ambler finished reading the announcements, she started pleading with us to bring more cans for the Thanksgiving food drive.

I looked over at Marissa and mouthed, "What's in there?"

Trouble is, before Marissa could mouth back an answer, I hear, "Meeeeow!"

Mrs. Ambler stops talking a moment, then shakes her head and says, "Anyway," and goes back to explaining the importance of the Thanksgiving food drive.

Heather does it again—"Meeeeow!"—and this time everyone laughs.

Mrs. Ambler looks around. "There's nothing humorous about hunger, people. I'm sure you can do better than this." She toes the cardboard box with all of four cans in it and says, "Everybody, and I mean *everybody*, is to bring in a can of food tomorrow or there'll be detention to serve!" Then she goes back to her desk to sort through papers.

So while the rest of us are getting books out of our desks for our morning classes, Marissa zips open her bag and pulls out a mitt. Not my mitt, but a really good-looking catcher's mitt.

Mrs. Ambler would kill her if she tossed it across the room to me, so I decide to sneak over and get it myself. But right as I'm coming up Marissa's aisle, Mrs. Ambler spots me. "Sammy! You know the rules. In your seat until the bell rings."

"Can I just—"

"*Now,* Samantha. Move it!"

So I turn around, and as I'm heading back to my seat, who do I see half out of her desk, looking like a tabby with her tail caught in the door? Heather. She's seen the mitt, too, only she doesn't know it's not mine. And she's busy thinking, How can that *be?* when the bell rings and everyone goes stampeding to their first-period class.

When I meet up with Marissa and Holly outside of homeroom, Marissa hands me the mitt and says, "Take good care of this. It's Brandon's."

I whisper, *"Brandon's?"*

"Yeah. He used to play youth league before he started swimming."

I slip my hand into it and say, "Wow! It fits great!" But it feels strange to be wearing Brandon's mitt. I mean, a mitt's not like shoes or shirts. Most people have lots of shoes and shirts, but if they have a mitt at all, they're only going to have the one. It's personal.

And standing there with my hand inside Brandon's glove, all of a sudden my arm prickles with goose bumps because it almost feels like Brandon's holding my hand.

I take the glove off real fast, zip it into my backpack, and say, "Thanks, Marissa. I won't let it out of my sight."

She says, "*And* I've got a great idea for the game. I want to go over it at lunch with you and Dot, okay?"

I say, "Great!" and then off we run to class before we get nailed with a tardy.

When lunchtime rolls around, Dot's already at the table sipping her root beer when Holly and I show up. And when Marissa comes scooting down the bench, she doesn't have her usual hamburger and fries—she's got a notebook and pencils. She sits down and says, "Have you been getting the feel of Brandon's mitt? Does it fit okay?"

Now, I'm trying to figure out a way to get around telling her that the feel of Brandon's mitt is too scary to even put on, let alone play a game with, when I notice that Monet Jarlsberg is sitting right behind me. I put a finger up to my lips, and as I'm writing, *Monet's here—let's go over the* wrong *signals,* I'm saying, "So what signals are we using tomorrow? Same as last game?"

Marissa bites her lip a second, then says, "No. I think we should redo all of them. Let's go alphabetical for the first signal—one finger for a change-up, two for a curve, three for a drop, and four for a fastball."

"That's easy,"

Dot says, "Got it!"

"Then for the second signal—one for inside, two for down the middle, and three for outside."

"Alphabetical again."

Marissa says, "Right. And Sammy, if you think there's going to be a steal, windmill your arm like you're loosening it up."

So far we're all doing a real good job keeping straight faces, but when Marissa says, "That's it for now. Just remember not to tell anyone about my arm. I kind of threw it out yesterday and I don't think I'll be able to throw any curves at all," we all have the hardest time not cracking up.

After that we get real busy talking about nothing, and the minute Monet sneaks off, Marissa starts laughing so hard she has to wipe the tears away. When she finally catches her breath, she says, "What a great idea—what a *great* idea!"

Holly whispers, "What is going *on?*"

So I explain to her about Monet Jarlsberg, Spy for Hire, and when I'm done, she says, "I feel like I'm in the middle of a war zone. This is crazy!"

I laugh, "Welcome to junior high."

It doesn't take long for Marissa to get serious again, only this time we get down the *real* signals and then we all huddle in to hear her big idea for the game. And when we've hashed it through, she says, "I'll talk to Ms. Rothhammer after school today and see if she thinks it's legal."

By the time lunch was over, I was actually feeling pretty good. I had a decent mitt to play with, we had a great secret weapon worked out, and Monet Jarlsberg was out there spreading the wrong information.

My good mood did a U-turn when I walked into science.

153

Heather was cocked and waiting, and when I came through the door she let fire with, "Meeeeeeeow!" And she must've been warming up the class before I walked in, because they didn't just cover their mouths and snicker, they completely busted up.

So while my rosy little cheeks are burning a path to my seat, it hits me that the reason Heather's back to being so cocky is that not only had Monet heard the stuff we'd wanted her to hear, she'd also heard Marissa ask me if I liked Brandon's mitt.

Either that, or she'd gone and checked where she'd stashed mine and it was still there.

And thinking about Heather having my mitt—about Heather putting her sneaky little hand inside *my* mitt—made me so mad I could hardly breathe, let alone concentrate on Mr. Pence explaining the miracle of mitochondria.

When class was finally over, I got out of there as fast as I could, but does Heather just let me go? No way. She calls down the hall, "Poor little kitten, can't find her mitten! Meeeeow!"

No one had to tell me to run along when school was over. I was down the steps and out the gate before the bell was done ringing. Holly and Dot came running up calling, "Hey, Sammy! Wait up!" but I couldn't talk to them. All I could think about was Heather having my mitt—my *father's* mitt—and how I might never see it again. I didn't want to talk about it. I didn't want to *think* about it. I just wanted to get it back.

And all of a sudden my nose is running and my eyes are overflowing and I can't see where I'm going, so I stumble over to the curb and sit down. And while I'm burying my face in my arms, Holly sits down beside me and says, "Sammy, what's wrong? What happened?"

I just shake my head and I can hear Dot whisper, "It's her mitt. It was her dad's."

I slap off the tears. "She'll never give it back. Never." Then I get up and run all the way to St. Mary's.

EIGHTEEN

I guess I shouldn't have used the side door, because Sister Mary Margaret jumped through the ceiling when I walked in. "Good heavens, child! Weren't you taught to knock?"

I'm in the middle of saying I'm sorry when I notice that what Mary Margaret's doing is counting money. Lots of money. Not hundred-dollar bills or anything, just lots of kind of rumpled tens and fives and ones. And I'm thinking that maybe it's money from Mass offering or something, but I've never actually seen anyone give a ten at Mass before. And there are *lots* of tens.

So she's standing there with her back against the table, spreading her arms out, leaning on her fingertips, trying to hide the stacks of money. And I'm trying not to stare or be too nosy, but it's hard. I force myself to look away, and say, "I'm glad you're feeling better."

She blinks at me like she's completely forgotten she was laid up with the flu. "Oh. Yes, thank you." Then she sighs, "Oh, this is ridiculous," and turns back to the table to gather the cash. "It's my bingo winnings, Samantha."

I say, "*Bingo* winnings?" because Grams has played bingo before but she usually only goes up or down a couple of dollars.

Mary Margaret stuffs all the money into an empty cracker box and whispers, "Indian bingo. It'll be our little secret, all right?"

I shrug and say, "Sure," and in my mind I'm picturing Sister Mary Margaret with a fat wad of cash, putting on dark glasses and a big hat, sneaking over to the valley to play Indian bingo while the rest of her friends play quarter stakes at the parish hall.

Mary Margaret clears her throat. "So, shall we get to work?" Then she notices the time. "You're over thirty minutes early. No wonder you caught me off guard!"

"I went over to the church, but it's all locked up."

"Oh, that's right. The Sisters." She shakes her head. "It should be interesting, to say the least. Are they ready, then?"

I shrug and say, "I guess so," and as we're going into the kitchen I kind of whisper, "You'll be glad when they're gone, won't you?"

Mary Margaret laughs. "It's like the circus has come to town and they're using our church as the big tent." She smiles at me and says, "I know they're here to help, but, yes, I'll be glad when they're gone."

We set up the food and clean up the kitchen, and when we're all done, we still have about ten minutes to spare. Mary Margaret says, "Could you open the doors when it's time, Samantha? I'll be back shortly."

"Shortly" turned out to be five minutes before the kitchen was supposed to close. And since Brother Phil never showed up and Sister Josephine was nowhere to be seen, I had to run the whole show all by myself *again*.

When Sister Mary Margaret finally does come back, she says, "Oh, Sammy, I'm terribly sorry! It was unavoidable. You run along—I'll finish up here."

When I walk by the church, I notice that the main door's propped open. So I go over and stick my nose inside, and there's Brother Phil at a card table with a strongbox and a stack of tickets. It looks like he's concentrating real hard on writing something so I walk up kind of quietly so as not to disturb him. Then I see that he's not *writing* anything, he's drawing, and what he's drawing on is money. I clear my throat. "How's it going, Brother Phil?"

He jumps and practically breaks the table in two trying to cover up the beard he'd put on Andrew Jackson. When he realizes it's only me, he rolls his eyes and says, "Give me a heart attack, why don't cha?"

I laugh. "Sorry."

He straightens out the table and says, "They giving you a comp?"

"A comp? What's a comp?"

"A complimentary pass."

"Not that I know of."

"I thought maybe after all the work you'd been doing for them they'd slip you a ticket. I don't think they're giving out *any* comps. What do they think? They're gonna sell this place out?" He squeaks around in his folding chair a minute trying to get comfortable. "Ha! That would be a first." He leans forward and whispers, "I think Mayhew's giving me this job just to see if the drawer'll come up short. Have I got a big surprise for him—every penny's going to be there. Every single one."

Someone walks in the door to buy a ticket so I say, "You show him, Brother Phil," and wave good-bye.

He winks at me like it's our little secret that he won't be taking any money from the box, and then says, "Tonight, tomorrow, or Saturday?" to the man waiting to buy a ticket.

I thought about Brother Phil and the rest of the St. Mary's squad for maybe a whole block. Then I remembered Heather and her stupid meowing, and all of a sudden I just wanted to be home. Home with Grams.

I get back to the apartment building as fast as I can, and after I sneak up the back steps and past Mrs. Graybill's door, I toss my backpack on the couch and run into the kitchen to give Grams a hug. When I'm done hugging her, she holds me out by the arms and says, "My goodness, Samantha. What brought that on?"

I kind of laugh, but she can tell what I really want to do is cry. She sits me down on the couch and says, "I haven't been able to stop thinking about that homeless girl."

"Her name's Holly."

"Of course. Holly." She sighs, then holds my hand and says, "Is *she* the reason you were asking me what would've happened if I hadn't been here to take care of you?"

I shrug and look down.

"Samantha, listen to me. Your mother would never have abandoned you. She would have taken you with her. At the time she just thought it was better for you to stay here with your friends."

"Oh, right! This is all a big favor to *me*."

Grams rubs my hand. "She'll come back, Samantha, and I don't think it'll be that much longer."

I jump up. "I don't *want* her to come back. I never want to see her again!" I sit back down and say, "I just want my mitt back."

"Are you sure Heather's got it?"

I roll my eyes, "Oh, I'm sure." Then I tell her about the meowing and how embarrassing it was, and how the thought of Heather putting on my mitt made me want to crush her into kitty litter.

Grams sighs. "I suppose you don't want me to interfere?"

"It wouldn't help. They've already checked her locker and Tenille's locker, and since no one actually saw her take it, what else can they do?"

Very quietly Grams asks, "Why do you think Heather wanted to take your mitt?"

I shrug and say, "To get to me."

"And why does she want to get to you?"

"You know why she wants to get to me! She *hates* me!"

Grams gives me a little smile. "And why does she hate you?"

I just shake my head. "I don't know, Grams. I was trying to keep away from her. Really I was! I just want her to leave me alone."

Grams pats my hand and says, "Samantha, Heather hates you because you always come out on top. You are a winner in spite of her."

I let out a sound like a blown-out tire. "Oh, come on, Grams! Heather thinks I'm the world's biggest *loser*."

Grams just keeps smiling. "That's what she *says*, but in her heart she knows it's not true. Think about it,

Samantha—in all the run-ins you've had with her, who's come out on top?"

So I think about it and say, "I have. But she always seems to turn it back around."

"And that's exactly what she's trying to do right now. Don't let her! I'm not saying stoop to her level—just get past Heather. And don't worry about revenge. Things have a way of coming around all by themselves. Sometimes it takes longer than we want it to, but in the end it always does." She pats my hand and says, "The way to rise above Heather is to play your best tomorrow *despite* what she's done to you. You're a winner, Samantha. Prove to yourself that she's inconsequential in your life." She gives me a mischievous little grin. "And if you want to hurt her more than she's hurt you, that's easy. Win tomorrow!"

I think about what she's said and it's like Grams has just put a little pocket of sunlight inside me. And the longer I sit there, the warmer I feel and the brighter things look. When she smiles at me and says, "Ready to help me fix dinner?" I get up and say, "Sure."

At dinner I ate all my rice and peas and didn't even try to slip Dorito any of my fish. And when bedtime rolled around I snuggled up on the couch and lay there in the dark, thinking about the things Grams had said. Then I reached over and pulled up my backpack, and just sat there for the longest time with it in my lap.

Finally, I zipped it open and took out Brandon's mitt. At first I just stared at it, thinking. About my dad, about my mitt. About where in the world both of them were while I was sitting up in the middle of the night thinking about them.

Then I thought about Brandon and how getting goose-bumps over his mitt was the stupidest thing my arm had ever done. Well, except for the time it went and waved at a guy stealing money out of a hotel room, but that's another story.

I mean, Brandon had probably just tossed Marissa the mitt and said something like, "Here, she can use mine," without even thinking about it. He'd probably lent it out lots of times—it was no big deal. Especially to a hotshot swimmer like Brandon.

Then I thought about the first game and about how maybe, with Marissa's secret play and a little luck, we could pull it off again.

So I got down to business. I put on Brandon's mitt. I pushed and flexed and tightened it until it felt really comfortable. And I guess I fell asleep working the mitt because when I woke up in the morning, I was still wearing it, only I was using it more like a Teddy bear than a softball glove.

And for once Grams didn't have to beg me to get up. I knew it was time. Time to go to school. Time to look the beast square in the eye.

Time to play ball.

NINETEEN

On the one day you'd expect Marissa to do the McKenze dance nonstop, she didn't do it at all. Not once. And any time Dot or I would say something like, "Hey, maybe Emiko'll come down with the flu," or "I hope the field's dried up some," she'd say, "It doesn't matter. Either way, we're going to win."

And if Dot or I would laugh and say, "Right, Marissa," her eyes would pop open and she'd say, "Get this through your heads—*we are going to win!*" so that by the end of the day we weren't wishing for a dry field or a sick pitcher, we were feeling kind of giddy. Like we were going to win.

Of course, that was before we were lacing up our cleats and Heather got her whole team to meow through a verse of "Where, Oh Where, Has My Little Dog Gone?"

Marissa whispers, "Ignore them, Sammy. They're trying to psych you out."

Now, I'm trying. But there they are, across the locker room, tossing their gloves in the air, meowing away, *laughing*. And it's hard. Real hard.

Finally, Ms. Rothhammer comes out of her office and says, "What's going on out here?" and you can tell from the way her hands are on her hips that she knows Mr. Vince's team's not just warming up for Cat Choir.

Everyone gets busy retying their cleats and pulling up their socks—everyone except Marissa. And she's about to step forward and tell Ms. Rothhammer what's been going on, but I grab her jersey and give her a shut-up-or-you're-dead look, and after a minute Ms. Rothhammer says, "Well, get out there and do something useful. Go warm up."

On the way out to the field Ms. Rothhammer corrals all of us away from Mr. Vince's team. "Okay, girls, listen up. I've checked out Marissa's play, the Fake, and she's right—it *is* legal. The signal I'll use when I want you to do it is this." She crosses both arms over her chest with her fingers touching her collarbones.

Marissa says, "Great! This is going to work, guys. They won't know what hit them."

Now, Dot and I are excited, but the eighth graders just kind of grumble and start walking again. Marissa catches up to them and says, "Hey, you guys, come on. I know you don't think we should be on your team, but—"

Before she can finish, Dawn Wilson says, "Darn right. You guys choked last game. If it wasn't for you—"

I'm sure Dawn thought Ms. Rothhammer was far enough away that she couldn't hear what was going on, but she was wrong. Ms. Rothhammer makes a beeline straight to Dawn and says, "I have had *enough* of this. If it weren't for these three, you eighth graders would never have won the first game! They're on this team because they're good. They're real good. And I'm tired of seeing the rest of you ostracize them just because they're seventh graders!"

Becky Bork kind of mumbles under her breath, "If they're so good, why'd we get slaughtered last game?"

Ms. Rothhammer leans in. "That's in the past. Today is what matters, and where these three are concerned you've got nothing to worry about. Sammy's got a good mitt, she's focused; Marissa's one of the best pitchers I've ever seen; and if Dot were any faster, they'd want to haul her off to do some bio testing."

That makes everyone chuckle, and when we're all done laughing, Ms. Rothhammer smiles and says, "Winning *isn't* everything, but in this case I think it's pretty important." She glances over at Mr. Vince laughing it up with the girls on his team. "For a lot of reasons." Then she says, "Look, you're a team. Individual effort is important, but no one player can win or lose this game. It's up to *all* of you. Now, get out there and warm those bodies up!"

So we start trotting around the field, the eighth graders in front and the three of us bringing up the rear. Marissa says, "Pick an eighth grader, any eighth grader."

I say, "Why?"

"Just pick one."

I say, "Okay—Jennifer."

Dot says, "Kris."

Marissa says, "I'll take Xandi. Catch up and run with them. Talk about anything. Just be nice!"

Dot and I look at each other and shrug, and then put on the steam to catch up with our eighth graders. When Jennifer figures out that I'm running *with* her, she gives me a what-are-you-doing-weirdo? kind of look, and rolls her eyes at Cindy Salazar who's beside her.

I just say, "Hi," and keep on running alongside them. I mean, I don't have any idea what to say to them—they're snotty eighth graders. But as we round the first bend, I try, "I'm sorry about Wednesday's game. I know I really blew it, but don't worry. It's not going to happen again."

Jennifer kind of eyes me like, Right, but Cindy pops her head out a bit and calls over, "What happened, anyway? Everyone said you freaked out because you had to play with one of the school's mitts. What's the big deal?"

I say, "The mitt that got stolen was my dad's."

They both look at me like, So what? and since I don't want to go into the whole thing about how I don't even know who my dad is or where he is, I tell them something that's almost the truth: "It's the only thing of his I had. He's dead."

They both look at me like, Ohhhh, and when we round the second bend, Jennifer says, "Well, maybe you should tell everybody that. Maybe you'd get it back."

I say, "She's not going to give it back. She'd rather eat *worms* than give it back."

Cindy laughs, then says, "You're talking about Heather, right?"

"Yeah."

"She doesn't seem so bad. Why don't you just—"

Jennifer cuts in, "Oh, Heather's no saint. She kisses up to us, but she's the one that Amber about killed for trying to steal Jared away, remember?"

Cindy says, "*Heather's* the one that did that?"

Jennifer says, "Yeah. And Amber probably never would've known if they hadn't played that tape over the PA system."

166

We're coming around the last bend and Jennifer says, "What I never figured out was, Who played the tape? Everyone kept telling me to look for a girl in green shoes, but I never saw her." She looks at Cindy. "Do you know who it was?"

"I just know it was some seventh grader."

Jennifer looks at me. "Do *you* know?"

Maybe I should've just lied, but I couldn't help it, I nodded.

By now we've stopped running and we're lining up for stretches. They both look at me like a couple of owls. *"Who?"*

I reach for the sky with the rest of the team while Miss Pitt counts off. "It was me."

"You?"

I nod, and the whole time we're stretching they keep looking over at me, shaking their heads and grinning. And the minute we get to throw the balls around to warm our arms up, the two of them run off to Kris and Dawn and Becky to spread the juice.

And the funny thing is, by the time Ms. Rothhammer comes back with the news that we're up first, we're like a different group of people. Becky Bork makes me give her a high-five and says, "I can't believe that was you!" Dawn says, "Yeah, and you couldn't have done it to a better person—that Heather is such a snot. She thinks she's the hottest shortstop in history."

I laugh and say, "That's what everyone says about *you*, Dawn," which a week ago would've gotten me blacklisted for life. Instead, what happens is Xandi and Cindy start laughing and say, "Yeah, Dawn, take it down a notch, would you?" and pretty soon we're all laughing and calling each other names. And for the first time since we started playing together it doesn't feel like I'm just a splinter on an eighth-grade bench. I feel like part of the team.

And when Miss Pitt rounds us up and puts her hand in the center, we all pile ours on top and yell, "Go! Fight! Win!" like we're really going to.

When Dot gets up to bat and I'm on deck warming up, I can hear Babs heckling her with, "Easy out, eeeeeasy out," and "It's a swing and a trip!"

But Dot just steps out of the batter's box, looks Babs straight in the eye and says, "Eat dirt, Filarski!"

Mr. Caan calls, "Girls! Girls! Come on, play ball!" so Dot steps up to the plate, taps it a few times, then wags the bat in the air, waiting.

And when Emiko windmills her a pitch, Dot nails it right between Gisa and Heather, out to left field.

Now, Anita fields the ball just fine, but instead of getting the ball into second, she tries to throw it all the way to first. The minute Miss Pitt sees what Anita's doing, she starts jumping up and down, yipping at Dot to go to second base.

So Dot curves around, tagging the inside corner of first, and by the time Julie's got the ball, Dot's halfway to second.

Monet's not standing to the side of second or even straddling the bag like she's supposed to be. She's planted right in front of the base, blocking it. And since Julie's winding up for a throw from first, Dot has to slide to make it, and she needs to tag the base, not Monet.

I would've just knocked her over. Really I would've.

But Dot's too nice for that. What she does instead is run a little bit to the side, and when she goes down for the slide, she sticks her foot out so it hooks around Monet and catches the bag.

The ball comes in right after, and while the crowd's going crazy chanting, "Dot-Dot-Dot! Dot-Dot-Dot!" she's slapping mud off her jersey, grinning away.

So it's my turn to bat, and let me tell you, I'm ready to whack the stitches open on that ball. But I look over and there's Ms. Rothhammer, with one arm across her stomach and the other one propped on it, rubbing an eye. In other words, I can't go whacking any stitches off the ball. I've got to bunt.

And then floating through the air like gas from a sulfur pit comes, "Meeeeow! Meeeeow! Meeeeow!"

I try ignoring it, but pretty soon Babs is picking it up, saying, "Meeeeow, meeeeow, meeeeow!" through her mask, and it's hard to concentrate.

So I step out of the box and look up at the sky, just trying to get my composure back. Then I look at the crowd, and there's Grams, standing by Hudson, right up front. She waves and Hudson cups his mouth and calls, "Go get 'em, Sammy!"

So I step up to the plate. And the other team's still meowing out there, but in my mind Grams' voice blocks it out. It's like she's standing there, whispering in my ear, "Rise above Heather....You're a *winner*, Samantha. She is inconsequential in your life." Then I can practically see that mischievous grin she'd given me, and I know what I have to do.

I look up, and there's Miss Pitt out by first base with an arm across her body, scrubbing an eye like she's trying to bury a contact lens. I smile and nod at her, and then step up to the plate.

The first two pitches are balls, so I let them go by, and then just to fake out Mr. Vince's team, I take a high swing at the next pitch for my first strike.

Now, Miss Pitt doesn't know I missed on purpose so she gets busy grinding away at her contact lens again. I nod, and when the next pitch comes in, I slide the bat sideways and bunt.

And I *almost* made it to first base. Trouble is, softball's not horseshoes and before you know it I'm out and heading back to the bench. I didn't mind, though. Dot was safe on third, and getting her there was the whole point of having me bunt.

Xandi was up next, and after every pitch she'd step out of the box. I don't know if she did it on purpose or if she was just so bugged by Babs that she needed to count to ten between pitches, but for whatever reason, it wound up throwing *Emiko* off. She walked her, which is something I don't think I've ever seen Emiko do before.

So Dot's on third and Xandi's on first, and it's Becky Bork's turn to bat. And I guess she was hoping for another change-up to slam into outer space, because she tucked that bottom lip in and waited. And waited and waited and waited. And when Mr. Caan finally calls out, "Steeerike three!" she just stands there for a minute wagging that bat like she's still waiting for the perfect pitch.

That brings Marissa to bat. Two on and two out, and

Marissa knows that it's up to her to bring Dot in. She takes the bat, taps the plate, and waits. And when the first pitch comes in she holds back and Mr. Caan calls, "Steeerike!" and puts up a finger. The next pitch it's the same thing. Mr. Caan puts up two fingers, "Steeerike!" Marissa's not tapping the plate. She's not even blinking. She's just staring Emiko down, waiting. And when Emiko finally zips her the next pitch, it's dead center. Now, we're all frozen on the bench, kind of holding our breath, because Dot's already halfway home on her lead and Marissa looks like she's just going to let the pitch go by.

Then all of a sudden she digs in and swings. And when she connects, half the school—plus a handful of eighth graders on our bench—jumps up and cheers. Marissa makes it to first and Dot scores our first run. None of us even cared that Kris Zilli got up next and struck out. We were too busy jumping up and down—we were *winning*.

But 1–0 isn't much of a lead. Especially not against a team that would do anything to win.

TWENTY

I didn't count the stitches on Brandon's mitt. I didn't even try talking to it. I just got down and sweated through the innings one by one. Brandon was about the farthest thing from my mind. Until the bottom of the sixth inning, that is. That's when I saw him in the crowd yelling his brains out.

I couldn't quite believe it. I mean, he was supposed to be at his school, what was he doing at mine? But it was him all right with his shiny swimmer hair and November tan. I wanted to wave at him and thank him for loaning me his mitt, but that'd be kind of embarrassing in front of the whole school.

So I tried to just ignore him and concentrate on the game. We'd been ahead by two runs at the bottom of the third, but then Dawn caught a line drive and hurt her hand, and even though she kept saying she was fine, she made a few errors and you could tell that she was afraid to catch the ball. Then Mr. Vince figured out that Monet's information was all wrong, and before we knew it, they were ahead, 5–4.

Now the bases were loaded, and since there was only one out, we were in some serious trouble. Debbie Wall was on third, itching to plow me over, Babs was on second, and Monet was on first, clapping her hands, yelling, "C'mon, Tenille, c'mon! You can do it! Bring us home!"

Well, there's no way Tenille Toolee's ever going to get an extra-base hit, let alone a home run. Usually she strikes out or hits an infield fly, which puts her out automatically. So I was glad she was up until I saw Ms. Rothhammer with her arms wrapped around like a support bra. And since her fingers are busy tapping her collar bones, there's no mistaking that we're supposed to use the Fake.

Marissa's getting ready to present the ball so I cock my head at the coach's box because I'm not sure she's seen Ms. Rothhammer's signal. Marissa nods, so I stand up and dust off the plate with my foot, and before I crouch into position, I make like I'm stretching and flash the Fake signal, just in case any of the outfielders missed it. Then I get down and call, "Any base, guys! Any base!"

For a second there Tenille must've thought God was smiling on her, because over the plate comes this easy little pitch that a tipsy turkey could've hit. Tenille hits the ball, all right. She pops it up, and Dawn catches it for an easy out. Then Dawn sends the ball back to me, and while the runners are sitting pretty on their bases, our team starts whooping and cheering, faking like it's the third out, not the second.

I throw my mask back and yell, "Way to go, Dawn!" and start trotting into the playing field. Marissa comes off the mound and all the infielders run toward her, jumping up and down, yelling like crazy.

The whole time, I've got my hand on the ball and I'm watching. Becky's charging from left field to cover third,

Kris has made it from center field to second, and Cindy is flying in from right field to cover first.

Mr. Vince's team is looking around like, What the heck is going on? and it looks like the Fake is going to be the Flop. Then Babs takes the bait. She comes off the base a few steps, yelling, "Hey, wait a minute!" and before she knows what's happened, I've got the ball to Kris and Babs is out.

Mr. Vince throws down his cap, "Get back on base! Babs, Debbie, Monet! Back on your bases!" Then he makes a beeline for Mr. Caan.

Mr. Caan comes forward shaking his head and says, "She's out, Coach. It's a fair play."

Well, Bug Brain isn't just going to stand there and get swatted. He buzzes around Mr. Caan with his arms flapping and shouts, "It's illegal! Show me where it says you can pull a play like that?"

By now Ms. Rothhammer's joined them. She hands him a rule book and says, "Show me where it says you can't."

Pretty soon Miss Pitt's out there with them and so is Mr. Troxell, and after about five minutes, Mr. Troxell practically drags Mr. Vince back to the sidelines. Mr. Caan calls, "Last inning, girls, let's do it!"

Our team goes crazy, whooping and slapping hands, and when Ms. Rothhammer comes over, she doesn't make us sit down and settle down like she normally does. She turns her back to the playing field, pumps her arm, and says, "Yes!" And it's as clear as the smile on her face—she's been waiting to put ol' Bug Brain in his place for a long, long time.

Then she gets serious and says, "Okay, girls. Keep your heads—we're still down a run, but I think we can turn that around. We've got them flustered, so use that. Annoy them with your leads, step out of the box if you want to. Take your time, but stay in control. At this point it's a mind game. Use your heads!"

We settle in while Cindy Salazar goes up to bat. Now, Cindy's a decent fielder and a decent batter. She plays well, but she's no fireball—she's more smoky. There's something there, but everyone's kind of given up on ever seeing it ignite.

So while Emiko's busy finding a toehold on the mound, Mr. Vince signals his outfielders to move in. What he doesn't know is that Cindy Salazar isn't just going to ignite, she's going to *explode*.

She measures up at the plate, like she always does, she holds the bat high and still, like she always does—but when the pitch comes in, she digs in and swings, and then follows through so far that she almost falls down.

I think she surprised herself as much as she surprised the rest of us, because for a minute she just stands there with her jaw to her jersey, watching the ball sail out to left field.

Miss Pitt yips, "*Run!* Cindy, *run!*" which makes her snap out of it and just *haul* out to first base.

Poor Anita had moved way in because Mr. Vince had told her to, and she's chasing the ball down the best she can, but by the time she's got a handle on it, Cindy's already rounding third like her cleats are on fire. When the ball finally comes in to Babs, the score's tied and Cindy's getting pounced and slapped and kissed by the rest of us.

So we're tied, 5–5, feeling like we can do no wrong when Jennifer Ryker gets up to bat. And what's she do? She strikes out. First three pitches—*swish, swish, swish*—she's out, just like that.

That brings us back around to Dot. And there goes the crowd chanting, "Dot-Dot-Dot! Dot-Dot-Dot!"

Emiko takes a long time presenting the ball. She digs in her toehold and flicks her head around a bit, and when she's finally ready, she holds up the ball, whips it around, and lets it fly.

Dot lets it go by.

"Ball one!"

Babs sends the ball back to Emiko, who goes through the whole ritual all over again—digging in, flicking her head, playing with the ball. And when it finally comes sailing over the plate, Dot lets it go by again.

"Ball two!"

Mr. Vince starts steaming. You can't quite hear him, but you can tell from the way he's pacing around that his mouth's warming up to yell some pretty juicy things at Mr. Caan.

The third pitch comes over, and it's another ball. Mr. Vince comes shooting over to the plate yelling, "What do you mean, 'ball'? You need glasses? It was right down the middle!"

Mr. Caan pushes back his mask. "It was inside, Rob."

"It was right over the plate!"

Mr. Caan puffs up a bit. "Coach, you do your job, I'll do mine."

Mr. Vince just stands there a minute flaring his nostrils

in and out, and finally he heads back to the bench and calls over his shoulder, "It was a bad call. You hear me? A bad call!"

Like he could really tell from over by first base. The bug brain.

Now, Dot doesn't want to walk. She wants to *run*. So she leans into the next pitch that comes over, swings… and misses. She swings at the next one, too. And misses again.

So she's standing there with a full count and the crowd's going bonkers with their, "Dot-Dot-Dot! Dot-Dot-Dot!" and she's primed to swing at *anything*. Only she doesn't. She can't. The next pitch that comes in is so far inside that she has to jump back to get out of the way.

"Ball four!"

Dot trots to first base, but she's not going to stay there long. She's going to run or steal or *fly*, but she's not hanging around.

I get up to bat and I'm busy watching Dot with her toe on first and the rest of her stretched out toward second, glad that Ms. Rothhammer's not making me bunt again, when over the plate comes the pitch.

Mr. Caan shoots up a finger and shouts, "Steeerike one!"

I forget about Dot and concentrate on the next pitch. It's low and inside, so I let it go by. Dot's already halfway to second by the time Babs gets a handle on the ball, and even though Babs bullets it to Monet, Dot's slid in before it's crossed the pitcher's mound.

The next pitch is right over the plate, so I swing. Trouble is, I hit the ball up the handle so it doesn't have a lot on it. But I'm not going to just stand there and watch Gisa throw me out. I drop the bat and run, and when I get to first there are two *smacks,* right in a row. First my foot on the bag, then the ball in Julie's glove.

Miss Pitt jumps up and down yipping, "Way to go, Sammy! Way to run it out!" and Gisa's over on third kicking mud around, spitting out four-letter German words.

There's no way Dot could've advanced, not with the way I practically gave the ball to Gisa. So there we are on first and second, and Xandi comes up to bat.

Every pitch, Dot and I would lead off, and every pitch, Babs would check us. And when Xandi finally does hit the ball, it's a grounder right between first and second.

Now, I've got no choice. I've got to run. And I've got one eye on second and the other on the ball, worried that I'm going to have to hurdle the thing to get to second, when I realize that since Monet's fielding the ball, it's not her job to cover second anymore. It's the shortstop's.

Monet could've made the out at first, but Heather's standing on second, screaming, "Here! Here!"

So what's Monet do? She whips her the ball.

I'm as good as out. I run as fast as I can, but everything seems like it's in slow motion—the ball coming through the air toward Heather's glove, me swinging my arms up to come in for the slide—and when Heather grabs the ball, well, the sneer on her face says it all.

But I don't slide like Dotty DeVries. If someone's blocking the bag, I don't go around them—I go *through* them. And it didn't matter that it was Heather in my way—I would've done the same for anyone.

And the fact is I did ram her. Hard. And when I did, she stumbled back, and out of her glove pops the ball, *thump,* onto the ground.

Mr. Troxell slices the air with his arms. "Safe!"

Heather screams, "There's no way! Didn't you see what she just did!"

Mr. Troxell shakes his head and slices the air again. "She's safe." Then he points to Heather and says, "You were blocking the bag."

Steam is blowing off Heather, but she doesn't say a word to me. She just hobbles back to shortstop, slicing me up with the Evil Eye.

So it's one out with the bases loaded. Our team's going crazy at the bench, jumping up and down, pounding on each other as Becky Bork steps up to bat.

Becky gets into her robot stance and waits. And waits and waits and waits. And when Mr. Caan calls, "Steeerike three!" she keeps right on waiting until Marissa finally goes up and taps her on the shoulder.

Talk about pressure. Two down with the bases loaded in the last inning of a tied game doesn't leave much room for error. Marissa measures up and waits, and when Emiko finally gets tired of checking Dot at third, she presents the ball and everyone holds their breath. Everyone but Dot. She takes a monster lead off third, and when the pitch finally comes over the plate, it's a good thing Marissa connects, because there's no way Dot could've made it back to third otherwise.

The ball nearly gives Emiko a buzz cut and goes sailing just left of second. Debbie Wall scoops it up on the bounce, but it's too late—Dot jets across home plate and we're ahead, 6–5.

Kris made the last out with an infield fly, but none of us even cared. We were *winning*. Even Ms. Rothhammer was jumping up and down. She huddles us up and says, "This is it...this is *it!* All you have to do is hold them. Just three little outs, that's all you need—just three little outs."

We all take our positions and when Julie Jaffers gets up to bat, she measures up like she always does, sticks her fanny out, like she always does, and half the boys in school whistle, like they always do. Then we get down to the business of trying to strike her out.

She waits out the first two pitches. One's a ball, one's a strike. Then she tips one foul for her second strike. On the next pitch she hits a line drive straight at Marissa, and *snap,* she's out.

Now, when Heather got up to bat, I don't think she was really thinking about softball. I think she was thinking about me. And when the pitch came over the plate, it wasn't a softball she was seeing—it was my head. She *killed* the thing.

For a minute there everyone thought she'd hit a home run, but Kris relayed the ball in from center field in time to stop her at third.

And while Anita Arellano's getting ready to bat, Heather's leaning toward home, pawing the ground like a bull ready to charge a matador.

Now, I'm not waving a cape. I just want a nice, clean double play and be done with it. So when Ms. Rothhammer decides she wants Marissa to walk Anita, I'm all for it.

So Anita's on first and Heather's kicking up mud on third, and Gisa's *jai*ing her way up to bat, when I hear something strange.

And it's not that hearing my name is so strange. When you're in the middle of a big game, you hear it all the time and you just kind of tune it out. But this wasn't "Sammy! Sammy!" like your friends do when you get up to bat—this was *"Sammy! Sammy!"* like "Help me! Help me!"

Marissa's about to present the ball, so, before it's too late, I jump out of the catcher's box and call, "Time!" Then I turn around, and there it is again, *"Sammy! Sammy!"*

I throw back my mask and look around, and there, six feet up the backstop getting yanked at by a teacher is Holly. She's clamped onto the chain link with one hand and in her other hand she's got a catcher's mitt.

My catcher's mitt.

At first I just stood there with my mouth open. Mr. Caan says, "What's going on?"

I call, "I'll be right back!" and run to the backstop.

Holly climbs down and says, "They wanted me to wait until the game was over, but I thought for sure you'd want this. I'm not blowing it, am I?"

I want to plant a great big kiss on her cheek and throw her in the air, but there's this backstop in my way so all I can do is say, "I can't believe it! Where did you *find* it?"

She laughs and then whispers, "It was in the Dumpster behind the locker rooms."

"In the Dumpster?" Right then and there I promise

181

myself never, *ever* to say another word about Holly digging through garbage.

She laughs. "Yeah." Then she gives me a real worried look and says, "I know the game's almost over, but...do you want to play with it?"

I say, *"Yes!"* so she nudges her way around the backstop and passes it to me.

So I've got Brandon's mitt in one hand and my father's mitt in the other, and that's when I realize that I don't *need* my dad's mitt anymore—I've been playing fine without it. It's still real important to me, and I'm ecstatic to have it back, but I don't *need* it.

I look over to where I'd seen Brandon before, and he's still there all right, looking straight at me. I check the field. Everyone's watching me, waiting. And I figure I've got maybe ten seconds before Mr. Caan starts yelling at me to take my position, so I run over to Brandon and say, "Thanks for letting me use your mitt. I...I..." but everything I think of to say doesn't mean what I feel, and it all sounds so corny, so I just hand it over. "Here."

He grins. "Anytime." Then he puts it on his hand and says, "Although I wouldn't lend it to just anyone, you know."

I blink at him like a complete dufus, and then Mr. Caan hollers, "Let's go!" so I hurry back to being the team turtle.

As I'm waiting for Gisa to get back up to the plate, I notice Heather over on third, only she's not pawing the ground anymore—she's squinting and bobbing around, trying to get a look at my mitt.

So I show it to her. I stand up and hold it open and wave, and when she realizes what's just happened, her eyes bug out and her mouth drops and she looks more like a gargoyle than an angry bull.

I get back into position and when the pitch comes in, Gisa hesitates just a bit, then decides to go for it. She hits it, but because she swung late, she practically put herself out, sending the ball straight to Xandi on first.

Mr. Vince is yelling at Heather to stay put, but she's not listening. She's going for it. And when I see her barreling toward me, I straddle the plate and wait for the throw. Xandi sends it in nice and strong, and as Heather dives for the plate, I swing my mitt down and tag her out.

Mr. Caan jerks his thumb in the air. "You're *out!*"

Our whole team starts pogoing around, yelling, "We did it! We did it! We won!" Everyone but me. I'm still straddling the plate with my mitt in Heather's face, and she's just lying there, stock-still.

When she finally looks up, there's mud all over one side of her face. Except for a white streak running down her cheek.

Now, I'd never seen Heather Acosta cry before. I really didn't think she knew how. And even with everything she'd done to me, I couldn't just leave her lying there in the mud. So I did something I never thought I'd do. I put out my hand to help her up.

She snorts and shakes her head like I've lost my last marble, and the next thing I know she's walking off, spitting on the ground behind her.

It wasn't too hard to forget about Heather for the rest

of the afternoon. I got out of my detention for the day so I could be with the rest of the team when Ms. Rothhammer took us out for pizza. Dawn couldn't make it because her hand was killing her and her mom hauled her off to the doctor, but the rest of us laughed and told jokes and went over the whole game play by play. Then we started planning what kind of party day we'd get Mr. Caan to throw come February when we brought home the Junior Sluggers' Cup trophy. The thought of Heather spitting on the ground never even crossed my mind.

But that night as I was trying to get to sleep, she kept creeping into my brain. And I lay there in the darkness thinking about things coming back around. About Holly and my mitt. About Heather. And right before I fell asleep I got this funny little thought that, in spite of what she said about me and thought about me, maybe *I* wasn't Heather's worst enemy.

Maybe she was.

TWENTY-ONE

I didn't have dreams about the Sisters of Mercy dancing in the outfield or pitching giant marshmallows. I didn't have *any* dreams. I slept like a sloth.

Until the phone rang. Grams hurried into the kitchen to answer it, and I think she thought I was still asleep because she was keeping her voice down. Even so I could hear her saying things she would normally never say if I was around. Things like, "Your daughter needs to see you, Lana! She's feeling totally abandoned," and "On *Thanksgiving?*"

Now, I can just hear my mother on the other end, putting on a big act about why it's so important for her to be somewhere else on Thanksgiving, and lying there, I start thinking about last Thanksgiving and how it was just Grams and me and a roasting chicken. And even though it *tasted* good, a roasting chicken is not a turkey, and no amount of basting and stuffing is going to turn it into one.

Then I start thinking about Dot with all her brothers and sisters and how she loves Thanksgiving because of all the baking and cooking her mom does and how they load up the table so heavy it looks like it's going to break.

I also think about Marissa and how, even though her mom and dad don't do Thanksgiving, they always pick up a dozen designer pies and head out to some relative's house that *does* and have a big party with all the cousins and uncles and aunts.

And I'm feeling pretty sorry for myself by the time Grams throws up her hands and says, "Very well, then, we'll have Thanksgiving without you," and hangs up on her.

Grams tries sneaking back to her room, but I roll over and say, "'Morning, Grams. Guess it's just you and me for Thanksgiving again, huh?"

She sits next to me and sighs. "I'm sorry, dear."

I don't want her feeling bad so I say, "It's okay. I like it better that way, anyway," and before she can tell me all the reasons why I'm lying I say, "Speaking of food...I'm starving!"

Grams pats my hand. "I'll get going on some oatmeal."

Now, I don't feel like having oatmeal. We have oatmeal every day of every week. I want something else—something *real*. "Let's have eggs and a slab of bacon and maybe some toast and jelly for once."

She looks at me like I'm an enormous spider. "Eggs?"

"Yeah. When's the last time you had a couple of eggs and some bacon?" I sniff the air and say, "Wow, maybe Mrs. Graybill's cooking some up right now....Can you smell that?"

Grams sniffs like she really believes me. I laugh and say, "Grams!" because the last thing you're going to smell in the halls of the Senior Highrise is bacon cooking. Eau de vacuum and Lysol, yes. Bacon? Never.

Grams lets out a little sigh and says, "You know it's terrible for my cholesterol," but she only says it with half a heart. The other half's tired of pumping around soluble fiber and wants some *bacon*.

So while she's sitting on the couch kind of dazed by the thought of actually eating something that tastes good, I get up and call Hudson. When he answers the phone, I don't say, Good morning, or even, Hi, this is Sammy, what I say is, "Hudson, you got any bacon in the house?"

He laughs and says, "Sure do, Sammy. You in the mood?"

"Grams is."

Hudson chuckles. "I'll get the griddle going. Come on over!"

So the next thing you know we're over at Hudson's, having bacon and eggs. And even though Grams starts out like she's eating raw alligator, she winds up practically licking the crumbs off her plate. When we're all done, Hudson pours Grams some coffee and says, "That should fortify you for tonight."

"Tonight? What's going on tonight?"

Hudson grins. "You and Sammy are accompanying me to the 'Have Mercy!' show."

Grams puts down her coffee. "Oh, Hudson, no. You didn't. The tickets are expensive and those nuns are so... so *loud*."

Hudson flashes the tickets like Get-out-of-Jail-Free cards. "You can't get these anymore. It's closing night of what's supposed to be the best show to ever hit Santa Martina and you're going with me if I have to take you kicking and screaming." He winks at me. "Besides, when's the last time you've done something cultural?"

Grams practically sprays her coffee. "Cultural?"

She's about to inform Hudson that she doesn't consider pounding piano and blaring music to be civilized, let alone cultural, but I cut her off. "You got me a ticket?"

"Yup."

I say, "This is great!" and even *I'm* surprised by how excited I am about getting to see the Sisters of Mercy bust down the walls of St. Mary's in their sequins and sashes.

For the rest of the day Grams puttered around her room muttering about cultural events for heathens, but by the time she'd figured out what to wear, her closet was pretty much all over her bed and she was too tired to argue with me when I told her I was going in what I had on.

We got there early, but there was still a line halfway down Church Street waiting for the doors to open. And when we finally did get in out of the cold, I was sitting down maybe two minutes when Brother Phil comes thumping down the aisle with his hair all crooked and belly popping buttons, looking completely frazzled.

I lean out and say, "Hey, Brother Phil! What's going on?"

He looks at me like he can't quite figure out who I am, and then says, "Oh, Sammy! Hi." He comes in a step closer and whispers the best he can, "Those Sisters are everywhere. They keep flying in and out, bossing me here and there—no wonder Mary Margaret and Josephine don't want anything to do with them." He holds up a spool of white thread. "They asked for thread so I brought them this, but it's not good enough. They're demanding purple!"

"What do they need purple thread for?"

He rolls his eyes. "Who knows. Maybe one of 'em busted a zipper. They're going nuts back there trying to get dressed."

"Do you think they want me to help them?"

Phil's eyebrows nearly fly off his head. "*I* do! Go on! Let them boss *you* around for a change. Tell them I'll be back with the thread as soon as I can. Oh, thank you, Sammy."

So I say, "I'll be right back," to Grams and Hudson, and before they can stop me, I go to find the Sisters of Mercy.

When I turn down the hallway, I practically slam into Sister Josephine. I jump back and say, "Oh, I'm sorry!"

She just holds onto her heart, takes a deep breath, and then moves around me.

I call after her, "Do you know where the Sisters of Mercy are?" but she doesn't say a word. Not one word. She just points her cane down the hall and does a power hobble out the side door.

I knock on the door and right away Sister Bernice snaps, "Who's there?" like she's commanding troops to stand at attention.

I say, "Sammy," and two seconds later the door flies open and I'm face to face with a great big nun in black tights and purple feathers. She holds both my hands so tight that her ring feels like a little icicle against my fingers. She says, "Child, I am so happy to see you! Would you do us the service of keeping that Brother Phil as far away from us as you possibly can? The man is like a fly in the Lord's soup!"

I can't help staring. I mean, I'd only ever seen Sister

Bernice in a habit, and here she is looking like an overgrown peacock ready to do battle. "But *he* just said—I mean, he's out getting you some purple thread."

Sister Abigail adjusts her tights, then bats down a few feathers. "I just hope the thread keeps him occupied until showtime."

Sister Clarice has got the same getup on, only she looks like a little purple chick compared to Bernice. She says, "Sammy, can you help me with my habit?" So I put her penguin suit on right over all those feathers, and then help the other two do the same.

When they're all set, I say, "I can't wait to see your show. I've never seen nuns sing and dance in tights before!"

Bernice laughs. "It's the shock factor—brings 'em in in droves. Like God didn't give us the wares to motate, you know?" She claps her hands and says, "Oh! I'd burn for eternity if I'd forgotten. The locket!"

Clarice says, "Better go get it now. I don't think Father would appreciate us waking him for our departure at dawn."

Bernice says, "I'll be right back," and as she's going out the door she turns to me and asks, "Is Father Mayhew still greeting people at the front door?"

"I don't know. Do you want me to go check?"

"Why don't you come with me? If he's not there, I don't relish traipsing through the church to find him."

But Father Mayhew turned out to be right around the corner, checking out the crowd in his church. Bernice comes up behind him and says, "Excuse me, Father?"

Father Mayhew jumps, then turns and says, "Oh! Oh, Sister Bernice..."

"I didn't mean to startle you, Father. Are you all right?"

"Yes, yes of course. I was just looking for Brother Phillip. Has anyone seen him?"

Sister Bernice laughs, "Oh, he's around!"

I say, "He's off looking for purple thread."

Father Mayhew says, "Ah," then turns to Bernice and asks, "Is there something you needed?"

She smiles. "I thought now might be a good time to get my locket out of your safe. I'm sure you'll be very busy seeing people off after the performance, and we have an early departure planned for tomorrow."

"Certainly," he says, and then looks back out at the crowd and shakes his head. "I wish I could pack them in like this on Sundays!"

Bernice laughs, and we both follow him down to his office. And the minute we walk through the door, Gregory comes wiggling out from under the desk and nudges me with his carrot.

I don't want his stupid carrot, so I scratch him behind the ears and say, "No, boy," but does that stop him? Not a chance. He nuzzles right into my leg and then nudges me until I finally break down and take it from him. He sits in front of me, panting and wagging his stubby little tail, and just as I toss it under the desk to get him away from me, I hear a choking sound come out of Father Mayhew.

He's standing by the safe with the door swung open, and when he looks over at us, his jaw's dropped down to his collar and he's just *staring* at us. I ask, "What's wrong?"

He swallows and whispers, "It's gone."

Bernice cries, "The locket? Someone stole the locket?"

Father Mayhew shakes his head and holds the locket out to her.

"Then what?" I ask. "What's gone?"

He chokes out, "The money."

Bernice freezes. "*Our* money?"

Father Mayhew looks in the safe, then back at us and nods.

Now, Bernice is heating up. Big time. And let me tell you—it's a scary sight. She's getting red around the habit and it looks like she's about to whistle steam right through her teeth. "Don't tell me that!" She snatches away the locket, plows her way over to the safe, and digs through some envelopes stashed inside.

When she's sure there's really no money, she whips around, points a finger at Father Mayhew, and says, "You! You're the only one with the combination to this safe! You said so yourself! I knew from the minute I laid eyes on you that there was sin in your heart!" She steps right up to him and for a minute there I thought she was going to strangle him. Instead, she just snarls, "You won't get away with this!"

While she's busy punching 911 on the telephone, Father Mayhew sits down in a chair and looks at me like he's just seen Satan. He holds his head in his hands and whispers, "How can this *be?*"

I sit next to him and I'm thinking, Yeah, how can this be? Then here comes Gregory, and *plop,* into my lap goes his stupid carrot. I put it on the floor, but he puts it right back in my lap, so I just leave it there while I listen to Bernice bark orders over the phone.

She slams the receiver down and says, "We've got to go on in three minutes, and I intend to do so! We've got a reputation to uphold." She points a finger at Father Mayhew. "I'll see *you* at the police station when the show is over."

Father Mayhew doesn't say a word. He just sits there looking out into space. And when the music starts he mumbles, "Will you excuse me, lass?" and walks out the door.

So there I am, all alone in a priest's office with a wall safe wide open and a clammy carrot in my lap, and I'm baffled. Would Father Mayhew really steal from his own church? Did he hide the cross and goblets to set the whole thing up? It didn't seem likely, but then the last few days I'd seen sides of him I'd never suspected were there. And he *was* the only one with the combination to the safe. Wasn't he?

So I'm trying to think, but it's hard because Gregory keeps nudging me. I hand the carrot over to him and that's when I notice something strange. The carrot's not like any of the ones Gregory's given me before. I take it out of his mouth, hold it hard between my hands, and sure enough.

It's still cold.

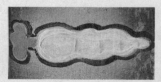

TWENTY-TWO

I didn't give Gregory the carrot back. I took it with me to Father Mayhew's filing cabinet and slid open the top drawer. Sure enough, there were still carrots in it. Room-temperature carrots.

I try breaking one of Father Mayhew's carrots, but all it does is bend. I do the same thing with the one Gregory had, and *snap*, I've got a piece in each hand.

Now, it occurs to me that maybe this carrot is poisoned. I don't know how you'd go about poisoning a carrot, and I don't *really* think it is, but I'm not going to give it back to Gregory. I give him the limp one and say, "Who gave you that other carrot, boy?" like he can answer me.

Then I sit behind Father Mayhew's desk and think. And I can hear Hudson telling me, "Keep your mind open, Sammy, keep your mind open." But at first nothing seems to want to come in. Then, very slowly, this idea comes tingling across my brain and down my spine. I look at Gregory and say, "But that doesn't make any sense..."

Well, I'm not going to sit there and argue with myself. I go back to Father Mayhew's filing cabinet, only this time I'm not looking for carrots. I'm looking for a file folder. When I see one labeled "Fundraiser," I yank it out and flip it open on the desk.

On top are letters of recommendation from St. Paul the Apostle Parish Hall in Lowell, New Jersey, and Holy Angels' Catholic Church in Haley, North Dakota, and then a really long one from St. William's Catholic Church in Santa Lucia, New Mexico.

Then I come upon copies of the forms Father Mayhew filled out for Bernice. Three or four of them were just forms with Father Mayhew's signature at the bottom, but then there was one with lots of blanks filled in. And on it was everything you ever wanted to know about Father Mayhew: Name, age, Social Security number, date of birth, driver's license number…everything. I took the form over to the wall safe and closed the thing. Then I spun the dial and got to work.

And in less than sixty seconds I had it open again.

Happy birthday, Father Mayhew.

My heart's bumping around pretty good, let me tell you. I mean, Okay, Bernice had him fill out the forms, but maybe they needed this information for something else. Besides, lots of people knew Father Mayhew's birthday. Sister Mary Margaret, for one. Josephine, for another. Even Brother Phil probably knew when his birthday was.

And Sister Mary Margaret had acted really jumpy— more like guilty—about her bingo money. What if she wanted more than just a cracker box of cash to take to Las Vegas with her?

And why had Josephine practically had a heart attack when I'd bumped into her earlier? Had she just come from this office? It was obvious she liked working with Father Mayhew about as much as she liked dealing with his dog, but more than that, maybe she was just sick to death of being a nun and wanted a way out.

And Phil. Ol' Brother Phil. Maybe he was mad enough at Father Mayhew that he'd actually frame him for stealing from his own church. It would do more than get back at him—it would probably get *rid* of him.

And I felt bad because it seemed like I was pointing the finger at everybody. And in the back of my mind I can hear Holly saying, Haven't you figured it out yet? You can't trust anyone!

But I didn't *want* to feel that way. I didn't want to point the finger at them any more than I wanted them to point at me. But *somebody* had taken the money, and if it wasn't one of them, who was it?

Part of my brain kept coming back to Bernice. Not because she was acting weird—she had seemed sincerely mad that the money was gone. And the locket *wasn't* gone. I mean, why would she steal the money and leave the locket? Why wouldn't she just take it all and leave?

Unless she was trying to throw the blame away from the Sisters of Mercy.

And I kept seeing Clarice putting a carrot in her blender. A carrot out of the NunMobile fridge. Father Mayhew's carrots were warm, the soup kitchen didn't serve carrots, and Sister Josephine and Mary Margaret's house was clear across town.

And Bernice's ring had been cold when she'd squeezed my hand. Like she'd just come in from outside.

Still, a cold carrot, a cold ring, and a fundraising form didn't seem like the kind of evidence Officer Borsch would appreciate, so I decided to go back to the changing room and dig around for something more.

The Sisters are in the church singing, "Give me peace... make me faithful now.... Give me peace... show me light! Give me peace... show me beauty now.... Bless me, Lord, take me to your side," and the audience is echoing their lines, so I figure as long as they're singing, I won't get caught digging.

I check behind a rack of clothes, *in* the clothes, in suitcases and duffel bags, but I don't find a thing. Not one nickel. And I'm just deciding that if they had stolen the money, the place to search would be the NunMobile, when I realize that the audience is clapping and making a racket, but the singing's stopped.

Bernice and the other two come flying through the door, and I'm in a panic because I just know they're going to ask why I'm there. But Bernice flashes me a smile and says, "Oh, good! You can help us with our next change!"

I smile right back and say, "Sure!"

While I'm stripping them down to their feathers and tights, I remember that Bernice had kept a NunMobile key in her habit. I watch them put on these wild purple headdresses, and as soon as they go sweeping down the hall like overgrown feather dusters, I pick up Bernie's habit and start searching for pockets.

I practically turn the thing inside out, but I don't find any pockets. Well, there's a big one on the outside, but there's nothing in that, and the day I'd gone inside the motor home with her she hadn't gotten it out of the big pocket up front. She'd kind of pulled it out of thin air.

I flipped it around some more and then decided that the best way to find a pocket—if there *was* a pocket—was to put the habit on.

So I got into the thing and it was like swimming through a mountain of black cloth. I groped around inside both sleeves, but no key. Then I closed my eyes and tried to reconstruct Bernie's movements when she'd been in front of the motor home. I put my right hand up the left sleeve, and just as I discover a small Velcro pocket up by the elbow, who comes busting through the door? Brother Phil.

He just stands there like an idiot staring at me, and I just stand there like an idiot, staring back. Finally, he says, "What are you *doing*?"

I give him a nervous little smile as I wiggle the key out of the pocket. "Nothing. I guess I...I guess I just wanted to see what it felt like."

Phil says, "Oh," then gives me an understanding nod and whispers, "I won't tell anyone." He hands over a spool of purple thread and says, "Here's that thread they wanted."

The minute he's gone, I dig myself out of Bernice's habit and duck out the side door. Then I race over to the NunMobile, insert the key, and let myself in. Just like that. I close the door behind me and lock it, and then look around. There's light coming in from the streetlights, and there's a little light on over the stove, but it's pretty dark inside.

I decide to start by searching up front. I go to the driver's seat and sit down, and it's like being in the cockpit of some luxury liner. There are switches on the armrest and levers all over the steering column, and there's a funny little TV screen by the side window. I put the key in the ignition and twist it forward so the interior lights will come on, but that's way too bright so I turn it back in a hurry. I put the key back in my pocket, then check all around the driver's seat. No money, but I do find a flashlight.

I go over to the passenger seat and check the glove box and all around the seat with the flashlight, but I don't find anything besides maps and papers.

The living room and dining room don't seem to have anything in them, either, and I'm about to move on when I remember Marissa talking about all the storage compartments in her uncle's motor home.

So I go into the dining room and start pulling apart the benches. Right away I find the laptop computer and a printer, and next to these is a brown accordion folder with a giant rubber band wrapped around it. I put the folder on the table and snap off the rubber band, and when I flash the light through the sections, it takes me a minute to figure out what I've found.

Mostly it's stationery and matching envelopes. But it's not Sisters of Mercy letterhead. It's stationery for St. Paul the Apostle Parish Hall in Lowell, New Jersey, and Holy Angels' Catholic Church in Haley, North Dakota, and St. William's Catholic Church in Santa Lucia, New Mexico.

And I'm thinking about Father Mayhew and the glowing letters of recommendation in his Fundraiser file, when I notice that the very last compartment of the accordion folder is kind of bulging out. I look inside it and what do

I find? Six lockets, just like the one Bernie had entrusted to Father Mayhew.

So there's no doubt about it—they're the Sisters of Sin. But still, all I've got is blank stationery, some look-alike lockets, and a couple of carrot pieces that are fast becoming room temperature. I needed to find the money. Or the goblets and cross. I needed to find something *real*.

So I start snooping again, only this time I decide to start at the back of the bus. I open the door at the end of the hall, and what I see is a giant bed with a wild purple bedspread taking up most of the room. I check out the headboard, which has little cabinets in it, but there's just hand lotion and Kleenex and some paperbacks in there. I check out the sideboards—same thing. Just normal stuff like clips and rollers and night cream. And I'm looking around thinking there's no place to store anything because the bed's taking up the whole room, when I think to look for drawers under the bed.

I flip up the bedspread and...no drawers. I run around to the other side and do the same thing. No drawers. And I'm just about to give up on the bed when something tells me to check under the mattress. I go to the foot of the bed, and when I pull up on the mattress, it flips up, and I find myself looking into this giant box.

I flash the light around inside and what I've discovered is the world's biggest pirate's chest. There's no money, or even jewelry, but there's gold. Lots of gold. There are gold statues of Mary and Jesus, of Jesus on the cross, of Mary praying. And I'm not talking figurines, I'm talking three-foot statues. There are dozens of plates and goblets, some with jewels encrusted around them, some without. There's silverware and *gold*ware, a couple of oil paintings mounted in thick gold frames, half a dozen ancient-looking Bibles, and over in one corner is a crystal chandelier.

This is not stuff you can go out and buy. It's old, it's gold, and there's no doubt about it—it's stolen. And tossed across a gold candelabrum like an old dish towel is Father Mayhew's cross.

I untangle it and loop it around my neck. And I probably should've just left right then to call the police, but I knew the money had to be in the motor home, too, and if it wasn't in the treasure chest, where was it?

I put the mattress down and started searching again. I checked the rest of the bedroom, the hall, and the bathroom and tried everything to see if it had a hidden compartment.

Finally, I was back at the kitchen. And that's when I remembered that Sister Mary Margaret had stashed *her* cash in a cracker box.

So I went through all the cupboards, digging through cereal and crackers and cartons of oatmeal. And what do I find? Carbohydrates.

And I'm starting to think that money or no money, I've got the cross and I've got to get *out* of there, when I open a low cupboard near the sink, and there, looking right back at me is the dial of a safe. That stops me cold. And then I remember how Clarice had come to my rescue when I was looking for a trash can. So much for sisterly hospitality.

Now, there's no way I've got time to figure out the

combination. No way. And even if I hadn't found the treasure chest and the stationery, the fact that there's a safe at all is proof enough for me. I mean, why would Bernice ask to use Father Mayhew's safe when she had one of her own?

I decided that the quickest way to get the police there was to find Bernie's cell phone and dial 911. Trouble is, I couldn't *find* the thing. I looked all over the front part of the motor home and it was nowhere. And just as I'm deciding to forget the cell phone and find a phone at the church, I look out the window and what do I see? A herd of nuns charging across the lawn.

I click off the flashlight, but it's too late. They've seen the light. Clarice and Abigail have their habits pulled up over their ankles, but Bernice isn't wasting time with that—she's coming at the NunMobile like a Brahma bull.

The first thing I think is I'm dead. D-e-a-d, dead. There's no back window or door for me to sneak out, and since I've just been through every room in the place, I know there's nowhere safe for me to hide. And watching Bernice coming at me, I decide there's only one way out of the mess I'm in. I've got to *drive* my way out.

I'd never driven a car before. Not even one of those little bumper cars at the fair. I'd seen Lady Lana drive and I'd watched the SMAT bus driver on my way across town, but I'd never tried it myself. So when I go up to the driver's seat and sit down, all I know is I've got to turn the key and push the gas. Other than that I'm like a turkey on a tractor.

So I'm flapping around, cranking the ignition, whispering, "God-oh-God, God-oh-God," when I hear Bernice rattle the door and yell, "Get me a key!" to the others.

Now, I can't sit down *and* reach the pedal *and* see what I'm doing. So I kind of stand on one leg while the other one stretches out to the gas pedal. All of a sudden, *vroom!* The NunMobile comes to life. I look over my shoulder at Bernice slapping at the window yelling, "Get away from there! Get *away* from there!" but I just pull the shift lever down to DRIVE and stomp on the gas.

And I don't go anywhere. The engine goes *Vroom!* but the NunMobile stays put. And I know any second Bernice is going to come flying through the door and turn me into turkey pâté, when I see the word BRAKE lit up in red on the dash.

I look around fast, and there it is, under the dash—the emergency brake. I yank the handle and *snap,* it releases the brake, and all of a sudden I'm moving.

And I mean *moving.* I hear Bernice scream, I hear this awful clanging noise, and when I look in the side mirror I realize that I've yanked the awning right off the grass and I'm dragging it along with me.

I can see Clarice and Abigail spinning around on the curb not knowing what to do, but I don't see Bernice. And as I'm bouncing down the street trying to keep from crashing, she appears on this tiny TV screen right next to me.

Well I yelp. I mean, even on a tiny TV, Bernice looks *big.* And I'm banging and clanging down the street trying to figure out where Bernice is and why she's on this little television, when I realize that what I'm seeing is a video of the back end of the motor home and Bernice is hanging onto the ladder, screaming her head off.

All I can think is, I've got to get her *off* of there. So I stomp on the brake, and then right away I punch the gas. She goes slamming into the ladder and then whips back, but she's still holding on. I try it a few more times, but she doesn't let go, she just keeps whipping back and forth, screaming at the top of her lungs.

Now, I didn't really have a destination in mind when I decided to hijack the NunMobile. I just knew that I had to get *out* of there. But turning onto Miller Street with cars swerving and horns honking while Attila the Nun's back there yelling at the top of her lungs, I know exactly where I've got to go.

I lay on the horn and cut across traffic, and believe me, people aren't arguing with me. They just move out of my way. I don't even wait for the light to turn green. I just keep on the horn and turn through traffic onto Cook Street. And I'm feeling like I'm getting the hang of this driving stuff, so I push the gas a little harder, and when I get to the police station driveway I turn and bounce straight in.

But as I'm bouncing in, a police car's bouncing out. And when they see me coming, they squeal to a stop, only I kind of panic, and instead of slamming on the brake, I stomp on the gas.

The NunMobile goes smashing head-on into the police car, and when I finally get my foot *off* the gas and the gearshift into PARK, the police car's pushed back a ways and the motor home's pretty much mangled up around it.

I'm looking out the windshield at what I've done, and

who squeezes his big ol' angry body out of the squad car? My good buddy, Officer Borsch.

I cover my face and say, "Oh, no!" and I'm expecting him to blow his top and start calling me names, but what does he do? He stands there staring up at me, and then starts *laughing*. No kidding. And pretty soon he's laughing so hard he's wiping tears from his eyes saying, "I should've known! I just should've known!"

Now I've got a hysterical cop in front of me and a crazed nun in back of me, and given the choice I'll take the cop. So before Bernice can make it to the driver's door, I scramble out the side door and over to Officer Borsch. Bernice comes staggering from around the back, looking like a penguin that's been spun through the wash. She gasps, "Arrest her! Arrest that girl! She stole our vehicle! She—" Then she sees how munched the front end of her NunMobile is and cries, "She *totaled* it!"

I try to stay calm and I say to Officer Borsch, "She's the one who's been stealing things from the church!" I hold up the cross from around my neck. "Look! I found Father Mayhew's cross, and there are all *kinds* of gold goblets in there. She's got a whole treasure chest in this compartment under her bed. And there's a *safe* in the kitchen, too. The fundraising money is in it, it's got to be!"

Officer Borsch is still laughing a little, but when Bernice gets in his face and screams, "Arrest her!" Officer Borsch whips his baton out and says, "Back off, Sister!" and let me tell you, he's not laughing anymore.

And I don't know if I was experiencing a divine intervention or what, but Officer Borsch looks straight at her and says, "This girl may be in trouble for driving your vehicle, but I've known her long enough to know that if she says you stole something, there's a good chance you did." He looks at me. "Which bed's the stuff under?"

I say, "The bedroom in the back," but Bernice yells, "Well, if it's there, she *put* it there!"

Officer Borsch turns on her and says, "Just stand there and be quiet! You'll get your chance in a minute." He backs up and reaches into the squad car, and while he's radioing for backup, Bernice turns around and gets into the NunMobile.

I don't know what she was thinking. The key was still in the ignition and she got the engine to fire up, but when she threw it in reverse, that NunMobile wasn't about to let go of the police car. She dragged it down the driveway a few yards, but we're in a police station driveway, for crying out loud, so pretty soon the whole mess is surrounded by men with guns.

Bernice didn't come out kicking and screaming. She stepped out of the motor home, put her hands behind her back, and waited. Like she'd done this before.

Officer Borsch sent some officers over to St. Mary's to pick up Clarice and Abigail, and I watched while they hauled Bernie away. And I have to admit I felt kind of sad. Maybe it was easier to see her arrested than someone who'd been at St. Mary's a long time, but I liked Bernie. Better than Josephine or Phil, or even Mary Margaret. For a nun she was funny. Of course, she probably wasn't a nun. She was probably just a crook. A funny crook, but still, a crook.

After they impound the NunMobile, Officer Borsch

comes up behind me and says, "I'm heading over to St. Mary's. Do you want a lift back?"

Now it's my instinct to say No, thanks, but then I realize that Grams and Hudson have no idea where I am, so I say, "Sure."

We go back to the police parking lot, where he gets in another vehicle and swings the passenger door open for me. After I buckle up he starts the car and says, "That was a brand-new patrol car, you know."

I look down at my hands. "I'm sorry. I…I've never driven before."

He gives me half a scowl. "Well, don't try it again any time soon, okay? You're terrible at it."

I look at him, and honest, I can't help it. I start busting up, because for the first time since I've met him I have to admit, Officer Borsch is right.

Completely right.

TWENTY-THREE

Father Mayhew signed off on my last six hours of detention. Said I'd done plenty for the community and didn't need to be serving any more time.

Bernice and the others, though, aren't going to be getting out of serving *their* time. Father Mayhew told me that Clarice and Abigail had a fit when they were arrested. Abigail kept screaming, "I'm going to kill that kleptomaniac! You hear me? I'm going to *kill* her!" And Clarice yelled, "You're the one who's always wanting to do one more town. 'Just one more town! Just one more town!'"

He also told me that they'd already traced back at least five towns where the Sisters of Mercy had been on their trek across the country, and it looked like there were lots more. He said in every town they used the same someone-tried-to-break-into-the-motor-home routine, and I guess they did such a good job framing the priest in one town that the poor guy was egged by his congregation as they hauled him off to jail.

Anyhow, Father Mayhew was so happy to get his cross back that he invited Grams and me to have Thanksgiving dinner with him and the real Sisters. And it's not that I was worried that Gregory would be pushing vegetables on me, it's just that Holly also called and said that Meg and

Vera really wanted me and Grams and Hudson to come to their apartment for dinner, and that sounded like fun.

So Grams cooked up a bunch of rice and baked a couple of pumpkin pies, and I put plenty of marshmallows on when I baked the yams so I could scrape the top and at least *pretend* to be eating my vegetables, and away we went, to have Thanksgiving dinner above the Pup Parlor.

When Vera brings out the turkey, we all sit around the table, looking at each other, feeling a little strange. Good, but strange. We're not family, we're just a bunch of people looking for family. But when Meg hands Hudson the knife and says, "Will you do the honors?" somehow it feels right.

Vera says, "I think we need to take a moment and give thanks." She looks around the table and says, "Maybe we could each say a few words?" She webs her fingers together, closes her eyes, and says, "Lord, I'm thankful for many things this day. For the food, for the company, but especially for the chance we've been given to open our home to Holly."

After a pause, Meg clears her throat and says, "Thank you, Lord, for all you've given us this year, but mostly, thank you for bringing Holly to us." She starts to say something more, but she can't. Her chin's quivering and she's peeking over at Holly, and Holly's smiling over her hands at Meg, kind of crying, too.

Then all of a sudden here it is, my turn. And I *am* thankful. For a lot of things. Mostly, though, I'm thankful for the people in my life that I can trust. For Grams and the way she seems to love me no matter what. For

Hudson and how he's always happy to talk to me and teach me things. For Holly and her digging through trash, and for Meg and Vera and how they take in strays.

And I want to list everything from Marissa and Dot to my high-tops, but I can't. I've got a big lump in my throat. So when everyone looks at me like, Well? what comes out of my mouth is, "I'm thankful that that's a real turkey and not just a roasting chicken!"

Holly cracks up and then Hudson laughs, and pretty soon Grams, Meg, and Vera are all shaking their heads and chuckling.

And if there is a God and he did happen to be listening, he's not mad. He knows what I meant, and I bet he's up there laughing, too.

Wendelin Van Draanen is a high school teacher, and when she's not instructing students, raising her two young sons, or running the family dog, she's writing about her favorite sleuth (usually at 5 a.m., when her husband dutifully drags her out of bed).

The first two books in this growing mystery series, *Sammy Keyes and the Hotel Thief* and *Sammy Keyes and the Skeleton Man*, have garnered praise for both their star ("Samantha Keyes is one tough, smart, resourceful seventh grader." —*The Horn Book*) and her creator ("Van Draanen expertly keeps all the subplots at a rolling boil while strewing the tale with red herrings, suspects, and clever clues." —*Kirkus Reviews*). Ms. Van Draanen is currently at work on the next Sammy Keyes mystery.